The Egyptian Curse

Another Adventure of Enoch Hale with Sherlock Holmes

Dan Andriacco and Kieran McMullen

Paperback ISBN 978-1-78092-776-3
ePub ISBN 978-1-78092-777-0
PDF ISBN 978-1-78092-778-7

Published in the UK by MX Publishing
335 Princess Park Manor, Royal Drive,
London, N11 3GX
www.mxpublishing.co.uk
Cover design by www.staunch.com

Dan Andriacco dedicates this book to

Roger Johnson

Kieran McMullen dedicates this book to

Eileen McMullen

CONTENTS

ONE
Death at the Opera

"To die! So pure and lovely!"
– Radamès, *Aida*

Enoch Hale watched the beautiful young woman die in her lover's arms, sealed up in a dark vault of an Egyptian temple.

For a few moments he sat in awed silence. Then, as the curtain closed, he jumped up and joined in the thunderous applause.

Hale had always loved the sweet romantic tragedy of the opera *Aida*, but it had a special meaning for him now that he had—in a sense—lost his own true love in Egypt. Ever since that day he had thought of himself, no doubt over-dramatically, as the victim of a kind of Egyptian curse.

"Marvelous," said the woman next to him, his companion, over the sound of hundreds of hands clapping.

Hale knew little about Prudence Beresford except that she had once been a nurse of sorts and that she liked opera. He'd shared an umbrella with her here at Covent

Garden a few weeks before after another British National Opera Company performance, *Madame Butterfly.*

"Oh, an American," she had said then when he'd thanked her in his Boston accent for offering to let him share her protection from the pelting June rain. "My father was an American. I met a lot of Americans during the Great War. I was a nurse and then a dispenser with the VAD—learned ever so much about poisons."

"Fancy that." After almost five years in London, Hale talked like a Brit at times. "I was a volunteer ambulance driver in France."

"That was very brave of you."

Hale shrugged. "Hardly. But it was more exciting than selling stocks and bonds, and it had the added advantage of annoying my family."

"What do you do now?"

"I'm a reporter for the Central Press Syndicate. That annoys them even more. My name is Enoch Hale, by the way. Perhaps you've seen my byline."

She hesitated shyly, and then put out a gloved hand. "Prudence Beresford. I'm something of a writer myself. Not a professional, of course. I dabble in fiction."

Hale couldn't help but think of his friend Dorothy Sayers. She had written a detective novel. It had even been published last year and she was working on another. Like Dorothy, Prudence wasn't a pretty woman, but she was almost handsome—heavy eyebrows, a thin but athletic body, golden reddish hair cut in a bob. She seemed to be about his age, thirty-four.

"May I buy you coffee or tea?" he said. "I really do owe you for keeping me dry."

"Tea sounds lovely."

They ducked into Frascati's at 32 Oxford Street. Hale had often lunched or dined there on the balcony, where the Belgian head chef Jules Matagne produced a modestly priced *table d'hote* with a Continental flair.

Now what? Hale was a bit out of practice at small talk with women. He hadn't been serious about a girl in two years. Dorothy didn't count; besides, she did most of the talking. Opera—that was a safe place to start.

"Do you go to the opera often?" he asked.

Prudence Beresford nodded and set down her teacup. "Oh, yes. I saw *La Bohème* and *Der Rosenkavalier* earlier this year. I come up to London quite frequently in my dear Morris Cowley." Hale gathered that she lived somewhere in the country and quite enjoyed the drive in her automobile.

"This is my first opera at Covent Garden," he said. "But I've already bought a ticket for *Aida*."

"So have I!"

"It's one of my favorite operas."

"Mine, too!"

At the time it had seemed only natural to make plans to meet at the upcoming performance of Verdi's Egyptian masterpiece. "And perhaps supper afterward at Simpson's in the Strand?" Simpson's was less than half a mile from Covent Garden.

"Yes, that would be lovely," Prudence had said.

Now, after the final aria of *Aida*, Hale wondered what he had gotten himself into as they walked toward the legendary restaurant. The woman was hiding something. Every time he tried to ask her a personal question, she turned it back on him without answering. "Where do you live?" "In my house. Where do you live?" He'd been down that road before, and it wasn't a journey he enjoyed.

Well, no matter. This was nothing serious—just meeting a friend at the opera, and supper afterward. She might as well be his banker friend Tom Eliot or Ned Malone from the office. With that relaxing thought he smiled. Prudence smiled back. Not a bad smile, actually. Hale hadn't seen it often.

"It's more than just the music I love, though that's glorious," Prudence said earnestly, slicing off a bite of Simpson's legendary beef. She wore a two-tiered pink, mid-calf length crepe georgette dress with tiers of fringe, and a purple and lilac cape over her shoulders. Her cloche hat was made of the same purple material as the cape. "I'm fascinated with Egypt. I even wrote a dreadful novel about it once, *Snow Upon the Desert*. Almost every Thursday I go to the North Wing of the British Museum and look at mummies and the Rosetta Stone. Needless to say, I'd rather be back in Egypt."

"Back?"

She nodded. "My mother took me to Cairo on holiday fourteen years ago, in 1910. It was a wonderful three months. We picnicked and saw the sights every day and I danced every night. But I didn't find a husband there, despite my mother's best efforts."

Hale almost choked on his beef. Didn't find a husband! That was too much. It had been a mistake to come here, he thought. He could never eat at Simpson's without thinking of the night that Sarah told him she was going to Egypt with Alfie Barrington—the man she later married. They had been sitting just two tables over from where Hale and Prudence were now. And Prudence's story had only rubbed the raw spot.

"What's her name?" she asked.

"Who?"

"The woman you've been thinking about while I've been talking to you for the past five minutes."

"Must there be a woman?"

Prudence sighed. "Mr. Hale, you are tall, handsome, expensively dressed, and gentlemanly. Yes, there must be a woman."

"You should be a detective."

"That's an unsuitable job for a woman, I'm afraid." She paused, chewing slowly. "But perhaps an amateur could perform the role—one of those elderly village gossips who know everything."

"Lady Sarah Bridgewater," Hale said, finally answering Prudence's question. "Or, at least, she was. Now she's Mrs. Alfred Barrington."

"Oh, I see. Married."

Hale didn't know what to make of her tone of voice. He shook his head. "No, you don't see. I wanted to marry her but her stuffy old father, Lord Sedgewood, wouldn't hear of it—never mind that the Hales of Boston and New York are richer than half the Lords of London. I wasn't good enough for the nobility. The Earl tolerated me as long as he thought it was just fun and games for Lady Sarah, but marriage was out of the question.

"Then she told me one night, right here at Simpson's, that she was going to Egypt for a few months with her father, and that her friend Alfred Barrington was going along. They were both into the Egyptology craze, the old man and Alfie—still are, I guess."

"You must have been very jealous."

"That might have been a man's natural reaction. But Sarah told me she'd known Alfie since she was a little girl. He was the scion of another noble family—the younger son of a duke, I think. She said he was just like a brother to her after her father temporarily disowned her real brother."

Hale took a healthy gulp cabernet. "Some brother! When I met her at the ship, planning to propose, she told me to meet her at the Criterion Restaurant. And that's where she told me over tea and crumpets that she'd married Alfie on the ship coming home. I haven't talked to her since."

The devil of it was that he could never figure out what made her prefer Alfie Barrington to him. Hale stood almost six feet tall, with light brown hair combed straight back, blue eyes, and a pencil mustache reminiscent of Douglas Fairbanks. Alfie looked more like a straw-haired vaudeville comic, barely taller than Sarah. Perhaps he had charms unknown to Hale. But Sarah had never actually said that she loved the man, had she? Maybe her father forced her into it, Hale thought for the hundredth time.

"You're a very romantic figure, Mr. Hale," Prudence said. "No one will ever replace your lost love in your heart. It would be useless for anyone to try. And yet you haven't approached her in two years, thus keeping temptation at bay, so you are an honorable man as well."

It annoyed Hale that she had sized him up so quickly and, in his estimation, so accurately. She was like a female Sherlock Holmes!

"You don't—"

"I only wish that someone loved me that much. Preferably someone quite as honorable as you."

And yet, Hale wondered whether she was married. She wasn't wearing a wedding ring, but her ring finger looked as though she once had. Divorced or stepping out? If she had a husband at home, or somewhere, that might explain her reluctance to say much about her current life.

Prudence picked up her purse. "It's been a lovely time, Mr. Hale."

"Enoch." Why hadn't he made the routine correction earlier? Had he been afraid to?

"All right, then." She smiled as she stood up. "I do hope that we shall see each other again at the opera next season—Enoch." She sounded like she meant it, but only that and nothing more.

"Don't you want dessert?" Pudding, the British called it.

"I'm afraid I really must go." She rushed off.

Was it something that I said? Of course it was. Hale smiled in relief as he contemplated having an after-dinner drink. He rather liked Prudence Beresford, but he knew now that he didn't want to get too close to her. He wasn't ready for that yet, especially not when there might be a husband in the wings.

Within an hour, Hale was at his flat on Claverton Street, near St. George Square. Later, he would tell Sarah that he'd been dreaming of her when the persistent ringing of the telephone woke him out of a sound sleep at three o'clock in the morning. He often dreamed of Sarah.

"Yeah?"

"Hale? It's Malone."

He woke up fast. Ned Malone was one of the top reporters at the Central Press Syndicate. Hiring him away from *The Daily Gazette* a couple of years earlier had been a major coup for the Syndicate. Best known for his news stories about Professor George Challenger, he was also an excellent crime reporter and a good friend of Hale. He wouldn't bother Hale at this hour unless it was important.

"What's happened?"

"I'm at Scotland Yard. There was a murder tonight outside the Constitutional Club. I think you know the victim—it's Alfred Barrington."

TWO
No Good News

Ill news hath wings, and with the wind doth go.
  — Michael Drayton, *The Barons' Wars*, 1603

"I'm sorry, Hale, but I'm afraid I can't help you this time." Chief Inspector Henry Wiggins nodded toward the newspaper on his desk. "It isn't my case."

The front page of *The Morning Telegraph*, one of the Central Press Syndicate's major clients in London, carried the headline **DUKE'S SON MURDERED OUTSIDE CLUB** across the top. Hale had devoured the story with his eggs and sausage before leaving his flat.

By Edward Malone
Central Press Syndicate

The body of Alfred James Barrington, 29, was found shortly before midnight in an alley off of Northumberland Street, just a few yards from the Constitutional Club. He had been stabbed in the heart by a knife, according to Scotland Yard officials.

Robbery has been ruled out as a motive, they say, as the victim had £67 in his wallet, as well as an expensive watch. Several persons are being questioned in connection with the murder, but no arrests have been made.

Mr. Barrington, the youngest son of the Duke of Somerset, was a long-time member of the Constitutional Club and had spent the night there, according to another Club member. His wife, the former Lady Sarah Bridgewater, was unavailable . . .

Far down in the story, Malone reported that the knife looked as though it were an Egyptian artifact or a replica of one. Hale would have put that higher in the story as Artemis Howell, a rival reporter at *The Times*, had done.

"Inspector Rollins has been assigned to investigate," Wiggins continued with a look of distaste on his normally impassive features. "That wasn't my idea."

Hale had formed a good working relationship with the wiry chief inspector over the years. They had frequently shared information on an off-the-record basis to their mutual benefit. Not many Scotland Yarders would go that far with a member of the Press.

"I don't know Rollins, but the name is familiar," Hale said. "Young, ambitious, and politically connected is what I've heard."

"Well, you didn't hear that from me," Wiggins said with a rare wink, although in fact Hale had been quoting the chief inspector himself. "But I'm surprised that Rathbone would let you cover this story, given your personal interest in the victim's widow."

That rankled, but Hale attempted to look surprised. "I'm a professional. My former personal relationship with Sarah is irrelevant. Rathbone knows that."

The truth was more complicated. Nigel Rathbone, the hard-driving South African who ran the Central Press Syndicate as managing director, had taken some convincing. He had wanted to assign the second-day story of the murder to Malone.

"Families like the Barringtons and the Bridgewaters don't talk to the Press, but they'll talk to me because they know me," Hale had argued.

"Perhaps too well?"

Hale shook his head. "I can be objective. Sarah got over me, and I've finally gotten over her." *Not exactly, but close enough.* "I haven't even talked to her in a long time."

"All right," Rathbone had said finally, tapping tobacco into his curved pipe. "You can get a head start on tomorrow's coverage and hand it off to Malone when he comes in this afternoon. Share the byline. You still have the best Scotland Yard connections in the Press."

Or so Rathbone and Hale had both thought.

"At any rate," Wiggins said, "good luck with Dennis Rollins, but don't expect any favors from him."

"I wouldn't dream of it."

"He's in his office. Been working the case all night. I don't think he ever sleeps anyway."

Rollins turned out to be a muscular man with a walrus mustache. His dark hair and swarthy complexion gave him a somewhat exotic and faintly foreign appearance. A rapid rise at the Yard—to the rank of inspector while not yet thirty—had inspired much speculation about his origins. The most common gossip had him the natural son of anybody from Winston Churchill, the pugnacious politician, to Stanley Hopkins, Commissioner of Scotland Yard.

Surprisingly, he greeted Hale with a smile that reminded the American of Teddy Roosevelt.

"So you're Hale." Rollins held out his hand. "I've been looking forward to having a chat with you." During the shake he squeezed Hale's hand harder and held it longer than necessary.

"I've heard a lot about you," Hale said.

"Doubtless. Have a seat." The official kept talking while Hale did so. "I know that you're cozy with Chief Inspector Wiggins. He's a good man." It sounded like a concession.

"Indeed. But I hope that you and I can work together as well." Hale pulled out his notebook. "I just want to get up to speed on the Alfred Barrington murder. I really only know what I read this morning in Ned Malone's story." Malone had called him before going to the murder scene, and before getting many details about the crime. Only with great effort had Hale resisted the impulse to fly to Sarah's side. That left him dependent on Malone's story for information. "Is it accurate that you questioned several suspects in connection with the murder?"

"Questioned, yes. Suspects, no."

"Then you don't have any suspects?"

"I didn't say that, did I?"

"Then you do have suspects?"

"I didn't say that either."

Rollins's expression was blank, but Hale couldn't help but believe that he was enjoying himself with all this wordplay to show how clever he was.

"Then which is it?"

"Neither, Mr. Hale. We have one suspect, and a damned good one."

"Do you mind telling me the name?" The question was a perfunctory one, asked without a hope of getting a positive answer. But Rollins surprised him.

"I should be happy to do so. You may quote me as saying that Scotland Yard is taking a strong interest in the victim's wife, Lady Sarah."

Hale's head jerked up from the notebook on his lap. Rollins's deep brown eyes were fixed on him, like a butterfly collector studying a specimen under a magnifying glass. Hale's mind was numb with shock at the totally foreign notion. "Sarah?" he repeated stupidly.

"Ah, yes, she is an *acquaintance* of yours, is she not?" The way Rollins stressed the word he might as well have said "paramour."

"How do you know that?"

"I've been learning a great deal about the Barringtons in the hours since I was called in on this case."

Resisting the strong desire to slug the smug Scotland Yarder, Hale forced himself back into journalist mode. He put his pen to notebook again.

"What makes Lady Sarah a suspect?"

Rollins sat back, totally at ease. "Come, come, Mr. Hale. One of the things I've learned about you is that you've reported on more than your share of murders. Surely you must know that the wife or husband is always the most likely killer." *But not Sarah!* "That's the first reason." He held up his index finger. "Reason number two"—the second finger—"the parlor maid, Mary Pritchard, stated that Mr. and Mrs. Barrington quarreled earlier in the evening and the mister left in a huff. Apparently that is why he spent the evening at his club." Another finger. "And reason number three, during this argument Mr. Barrington accused his wife of having a lover."

Hale felt an unexpected pang of jealousy, which made him feel foolish. What was Sarah to him now, really?

"Perhaps Miss Pritchard misunderstood her mistress," he said. That sort of thing happened all the time in detective stories.

"How does one misinterpret 'You love him, don't you?' "

Hale found it hard to believe that the Sarah he knew would kill someone, but she was no longer the Sarah he knew. Perhaps being married to Alfie had caused her to crack. "What does Lady Sarah say about all this?"

"She confirms that there was an argument—she called it 'a bit of a tiff'—but she said her husband was in error with his suspicions. After Mr. Barrington left, she had Miss Pritchard prepare a sleeping draught for her. Miss Pritchard stated that she watched her drink it. Lady Sarah was apparently still asleep when we called on her early this morning with the news of her husband's death."

Now Hale was confused. "Wait a minute, Inspector. You're saying that she has an alibi? That she was in her home sleeping when her husband was killed?"

Rollins nodded. "We believe that to be the case."

"Then how could she have killed her husband?"

"She didn't have to, Mr. Hale. Isn't that what lovers are for?" He straightened up in his chair and eyed Hale as he lit a cigar. "As I said, I've been looking forward to having a chat with you. Where were you last evening?"

THREE
Old Lovers

How miserable is the man who loves.
— Plautus, *Asinaria*, 200 B.C.

"You've got to be kidding."

"I am not noted for making jokes during murder investigations," Rollins said dryly. "But I presume that is an Americanism."

Why did I not see this coming? Of course Scotland Yard would suspect the wife, and of course they would look for a boyfriend—especially in the light of the argument overheard by the parlor maid. And Hale so conveniently fit the role, although he no longer played it. It was hardly unknown for a woman to continue a romantic relationship with a former lover after marrying another man, especially among the upper classes. That must have been why Rollins had been so forthcoming with news about the investigation: He'd been carefully watching Hale's every reaction to the information he laid out as bait. Well, there was nothing for it but to tell the truth. Hale had nothing to hide.

"It's true that I was once very close to Lady Sarah Bridgewater," he said, "but I haven't seen her since 1922."

"Not since the wedding?"

"She got married on a ship on her way back from Egypt. I saw her the day she returned, when she informed me that she was now Mrs. Barrington. That was the last time was spoke."

"Then you won't mind telling me where you were last evening."

"Early in the evening I was at Covent Garden watching *Aida*. Afterwards, I went out to supper at Simpson's."

"Were you alone?" He said it as if he expected Hale to answer in the affirmative.

Hale hesitated. Was it fair to drag Prudence into this? What if she was married, as he suspected? He didn't want to get the woman in trouble with her husband. On the other hand, there is trouble and then there is big trouble. Being questioned in a murder investigation struck Hale as big trouble.

"I was with a woman named Prudence Beresford. We were together from about seven o'clock to just after midnight."

Rollins adopted an ironic smile. "That's very convenient. I'm sure you know that Mr. Barrington's body was found about eleven forty-five."

"Yes, I know. I read that in the newspaper."

"What do you mean by 'together' with this woman?"

"Not what you think I mean. She went home from Simpson's."

"Where does she live?"

"That I don't know. Somewhere in the country, I gather."

Rollins managed to infuse the arching of an eyebrow with cynicism. "You don't know?"

"She never told me." Hale squirmed in his chair, knowing that this was going to be hard for the inspector to swallow. "Look, I only know this woman from seeing her at the opera. She's no more than a casual acquaintance. I've never been to her house or flat and she's never been to mine. We met up at Covent Garden and walked together to Simpson's after the opera. That's the extent of it. I may or may not see her again next opera season."

Rollins didn't say anything, just looked at him. Hale knew that trick because he had often used it himself as a reporter. Most people are so uncomfortable with silence that they tend to fill it with words, often saying more than they should. But Hale didn't do that. Silence hung in the air like an unwelcome guest at a party.

After perhaps a minute, the inspector said, "You do realize that's not a very believable story, don't you?"

"Of course I do. If I were making it up, I'd have done a better job."

Rollins grunted, giving the impression that he didn't think much of Hale's argument. "We shall see if we can find Miss Beresford. In the meanwhile"—he held out his hand—"I should like to hold on to your passport until this matter is resolved."

At about the same time that mid-morning, the widow Barrington emerged from a fitful sleep for the second time that morning—this time alone in the room. She sat up in bed. Disoriented, fragmented memories returned to her . . . Mary shaking her awake and then—

Alfie is dead. Everything has changed.

The usually attractive Lady Sarah looked much older than her twenty-five years, with her short blond hair in disarray and the fair skin of her face sagging. Her wide green eyes would have seemed dead, had there been anyone to observe them. She had once performed on the stage under another name and had even found a dead body, but this . . .

What a nightmare! That horrible man from Scotland Yard—not at all like dear Wiggins—seemed to have an endless supply of impertinent questions.

"Was it common for your husband to stay overnight at his club, Lady Sarah?"

"Is it true that you two had a violent quarrel last night that resulted in him storming out of the house?"

"And in this quarrel was something said about you loving another man?"

"Didn't you have a strong attachment to Mr. Enoch Hale before your unexpected marriage to Mr. Barrington?"

Question, questions, questions! She had wanted to scream.

Rollins had seemed to imply that she arranged for Alfie to be killed by Enoch. How absurd! Enoch surely would come to hate her for that, if he didn't hate her already. She had to find some way to get him out of this mess. But how? The only thing she could think of was to tell the truth.

And that was unthinkable.

FOUR
Leading Suspect

"Great is journalism. Is not every able editor a ruler of
the world, being the persuader of it?"
  – Thomas Carlyle, *The French Revolution*, 1837

Hale stood waiting nervously as Rathbone finished
reading his story. It could have been his imagination, but he
thought he saw the managing director's eyes widen as he
read the first sentence:

"Enoch Hale, a reporter for the Central Press
Syndicate, has emerged as the leading suspect in the
stabbing Sunday night of Alfred Barrington."

But Rathbone kept reading, puffing energetically on
his pipe. Finally, he looked up and sat back in his chair.
"You really have balls, Hale. I suppose you know that."

"I've been told so before, sir, although not always
so colorfully."

But he didn't feel very ballsy as Rathbone took his
pen to the manuscript and started writing on it. "What are
you doing?"

"I'm turning this into a first-person account by a
murder suspect, Hale. Your involvement in the story is
what makes it unique. We need to run with that angle, not

bury it: 'This reporter has emerged as,' etc. The byline will
tell the readers who you are and who you work for. Half the
newspapers in the United Kingdom will carry this story, and
the other half will carry stories *about* it. Well done, Hale,
well done!" That was about the most Rathbone ever gave
by way of approval, and any of his reporters would have
fought a duel to earn it. "Too bad it will be your last story
on this case."

"What do you mean?"

"I'm going to turn it all over to Malone from this
point, as planned. He can handle it."

"So can I!"

"But Malone isn't a suspect in the case."

Hale felt his ears get red. "Surely you don't think I
killed Alfie Barrington!"

"Of course not." Rathbone's eyes wandered to his
pipe, to Hale's manuscript, to the typewriter on his desk.
"However, er, just for the record—"

"No, I didn't. I was at the opera when he was
killed." Hale forced himself to slow down and stop
shouting. "That's in my story. And I was telling you the
truth this morning when I said that Sarah and I were
finished long ago."

"Right. I have every confidence in you, Hale. That
isn't really the issue, though, is it? You can't be reporting on
a murder in which you're Scotland Yard's chief suspect, can
you? Think about it, man!"

Hale thought about it. Rathbone's point made
perfect sense; he had to admit that. His name on stories
about the murder, even those that didn't involve the
Scotland Yard investigation, would put the Central Press
Syndicate in a position that was far beyond merely
awkward.

"I understand, sir. But when Scotland Yard finds
Miss Beresford"—was she really a miss?—"and verifies my
alibi, I won't be a suspect anymore."

"And when that happens, I'll put you back on the story to help Malone. Meanwhile, I want you to work on a follow-up feature story on Leigh Mallory.

"The Everest fellow?"

George Herbert Leigh Mallory, a 37-year-old mountaineer, and his climbing partner had disappeared on the northeast ridge of Mount Everest a little more than two weeks earlier, on June 7.

"That's right. By this time he's certainly dead and we've never told the whole story—aging mountain climber, last chance to scale the world's largest mountain, all that. I want the story on my desk by Wednesday morning. That gives you the rest of today and tomorrow, plenty of time to do it right."

Hale's alibi, the woman who had given her name to him as Prudence Beresford, read that morning's *Times* story about the murder of Alfred James Barrington with great interest. It combined two of her favorite subjects: murder and Egypt. In fact, it reminded her a bit of one of her own short stories. The article had been written by a man named Artemis Howell. She had paid a lot of attention to bylines since first meeting Enoch Hale a few weeks earlier.

Alfred Barrington, the son-in-law and close associate of Edward Bridgewater, the Earl of Sedgewood, was found stabbed to death near his club on Sunday night.

Lord Sedgewood and the late Lord Carnarvon, sponsor of the expedition that found the tomb of the Pharaoh Tutankhamun two years ago, were long-time rivals in the field of Egyptology. The victim shared his father-in-law's passion and traveled with him to Egypt several months before their competitor's fabulous discovery.

The death of Lord Carnarvon in Egypt on 23 April 1923 has been attributed by some to a mummy's curse, although doctors blamed an infection from a bug bite. It is said that as the peer died, lights throughout the city of Cairo . . .

Curse or not, she didn't like knives and guns. Death by poison was so much neater. Besides, she knew a lot about poisons. It was just possible the stabbing could add an exotic touch, though, if the weapon turned out to be a jewelled scimitar or some such. That would lift this story above the typical sordid accounts of robbery and murder that one found in the unimaginative daily Press. There was promise here. She picked up her scissors and clipped the article.

FIVE
Bedford Place

The less we know the more we suspect.
> – H.W. Shaw, *Josh Billings' Encyclopedia of Wit and Wisdom*, 1874

Rathbone could take Hale off of the story, but he couldn't stop him from visiting Sarah. Hale had been asking himself since that early-morning phone call how he felt about her. He had slowly come to admit that the hurt was still there—and so was the love.

After lunch, Hale headed for Bloomsbury. Sarah and Alfie had set up housekeeping at 12 Bedford Place, just two blocks over from the British Museum. It was a short street in a modest neighborhood of artists and academics, a little more than a tenth of a mile running between Russell Street and Bloomsbury Square Gardens.

"Yes?" The servant who answered the door, a tall man with an abundant mop of thick gray hair and a stoop, regarded him skeptically.

"I'm here to see Lady Sarah."

"I am afraid that Madam is not receiving visitors." He started to close the door, but Hale prevented that with a quick foot.

"I'm not a visitor, I'm an old friend."

"Nevertheless, sir—"

Hale handed the man his business card. "Just give her this."

"As you wish, sir."

As the door closed in his face, Hale worried that the "Central Press Syndicate" beneath his name on the card might cause the butler to throw it away rather than take it to Sarah. Or maybe Sarah would throw it away herself. That fear grew as the minutes ticked by. Hale began to feel foolish standing on the stoop, hat in hand.

Finally, the door opened.

"Lady Sarah will see you, sir." The stiff upper lip failed to conceal the butler's surprise.

Hale had never understood the reference to one's heart skipping a beat until he entered the parlor and saw Sarah. Sitting on a divan, flanked by her brother on one side and a willowy, red-haired woman Hale didn't know on the other, Sarah seemed at least a decade older than her true age in the mid-twenties.

"Hello, Sarah. I'm so sorry about Alfie."

"Enoch!"

She ran to him. The hug didn't last long; just long enough to tear Hale's heart apart. "That dreadful policeman asked me about you. How I wish you hadn't been dragged into this!"

"Tempest in a teapot. Don't worry about it. Rollins will be singing a different tune as soon as he confirms my alibi."

Charles Bridgewater stood up, and the other woman on the divan immediately followed suit.

"It's been a long time, Hale," Sarah's brother said as he presented his hand. "Good to see you again." Charles was still thin and still spoke as if he'd just arrived from Oxford, although he no longer wore a pince-nez on his aristocratic nose. Hale had first met him while Sarah was in

Egypt[1]. Estranged from his father because of his dissolute living after returning from the War, he had been working under another name. Later, Hale had heard that father and son had reconciled. But Charles had always remained close to his sister, even when that required meeting her secretly during the estrangement from his father.

"May I present my fiancé, Portia Lyme?"

She smiled and offered her hand. Bright young things always did that. And she was certainly young, perhaps twenty or so. Hale suspected she was the spoiled, thoroughly modern daughter of a minor nobleman.

"I saw the story in *The Times*—lot of rubbish about Carnarvon and the supposed Tutankhamun curse." Charles held up Hale's card. "I suppose you're here for more of the same?"

"Charles!" Sarah said.

"I'm here as a friend, not as a journalist," Hale said. "I'd like to help Sarah. But I think the best way I can do that is to act a bit like a journalist—ask a lot of obnoxious questions until I find something that might be helpful. At some point in the process I might want to pass something along to a colleague for publication, but I won't do that without your approval."

"What kind of questions?" Sarah asked.

Hesitating, Hale glanced toward Portia Lyme. She didn't look away.

"Portia's going to be part of our family," Sarah said. "Whatever you want to ask, you can do it in front of her."

Hale nodded. "All right, then. Inspector Rollins said you had an argument with Alfie last night. Was your marriage in trouble?"

"Now see here, Hale!" Charles sputtered.

Sarah cast her green eyes down. "No, it's all right. The inspector asked about that, and I'm sure he'll be asking

---

[1] See *The Poisoned Penman*, MX Publishing, 2014.

the servants and all of Alfie's friends. The fact is, we didn't quarrel a lot. But neither were we in love. I think I told you once, Enoch, that he was like a brother to me. That turned out to be all too true. We were more like brother and sister than husband and wife."

If Charles and his girl hadn't been in the room, Hale would have taken her into his arms. He had to force himself to pay attention as Sarah continued.

"I suppose it's only natural that he should look elsewhere for . . . female companionship."

"He had a girlfriend?"

"I'm not really sure." She sat back down on the divan, hesitating as she apparently collected her thoughts. "He'd been hanging around with what they call the Bloomsbury Group, the writers and artists that populate this district. I suspect he was rather too fond of that Virginia Woolf woman."

"Suspect or know?"

"It's just a feeling I have, and not a strong one. What difference does it make whether they were intimate or not? That's where he spent his time, that's where his heart was—with that crowd and at his club."

Hale had heard of Woolf as a writer, and a wild woman, although he'd never read anything by her.

"Isn't Virginia Woolf quite a bit older than Alfie?" he asked.

"Oh, yes—early forties, I think. Doesn't say much for me, does it?" Her cheeks flushed as she inspected her hands nervously held in her lap.

"And isn't she married to some sort of literary type—an editor or something of the kind?"

Sarah nodded. "Yes, Leonard Woolf. He was a friend of Alfie's, too. It was all very *civilized*." The last word was spit out with a heavy note of bitterness.

"Father was quite upset about Alfie's choice of friends," Charles said.

Was it almost as bad as your sister seeing a journalist? Lord Sedgewood's contempt for his profession still rankled Hale. He had chosen it in part to irritate his father, and was dismayed when it proved a stumbling block to his potential father-in-law as well.

Hale could think of all sorts of love-triangle murder motives that wouldn't make Sarah the murderer. Perhaps Alfie wanted to break off whatever he had going with Virginia Woolf—if anything. Or perhaps Leonard Woolf wasn't as "civilized" as he liked to let on.

"Do you think Alfie's involvement with these people may have had anything to do with his murder, Sarah?"

"No, of course not."

"Then whom do you suspect?"

"No one! I can't imagine anyone wanting to kill Alfie. He was so . . . inoffensive. I shall miss him terribly."

Sarah turned slightly, as though to hide the catch in her throat and the tear in her eye. Were they the products of emotion or acting? Given that she had once been a music hall performer, Hale couldn't be sure which it was. And he was even less sure which he wanted it to be.

"Even the governor wouldn't kill a man just because he didn't like the company he was keeping," Charles said.

"Don't even talk like that!" Sarah snapped, her voice trembling. Portia Lyme's air of youthful sophistication dissipated into a look of embarrassment. She looked like she'd rather be somewhere else.

Maybe Sedgewood *would* do that, Hale thought—not out of calculation, certainly, but out of rage. And maybe that's why Sarah reacted so strongly.

He thought back to the first time he had met the fifth Earl of Sedgewood, almost four years earlier during his reporting of the Hangman murders[2]. Hale had managed to

---

[2] See *The Amateur Executioner*, MX Publishing, 2013.

talk his way into His Lordship's oak-paneled library, where they sat and talked next to a black statue of the Egyptian cat-goddess Bastet. Convinced that Hale was in the pay of the Bolsheviks or his rival Carnarvon, the Earl had answered few questions before ordering him out of the town house. Their relationship had later taken several interesting turns—after Sedgewood found out that Hale was involved with his daughter and before he convinced her to go with him to Egypt. A widower, he was very protective of Sarah.

Hale made a mental note to check on where Sedgewood was last night. Then he changed the subject without warning, always a good interview technique.

"I didn't ask you about the quarrel you and Alfie had last night. According to Rollins, Alfie was overheard to say something like 'you love him, don't you?' I know what you told Rollins about that, but if I'm going to help you I need to know the truth. I'm also kind of curious since it's the reason I have to prove where I was during the murder. So let's have it: Is there another man in the picture?"

Sarah opened her mouth to answer. Hale would later wonder what she would have said if the door hadn't opened behind him.

"Daddy! What did he say?"

The peer, a short man with a bit of a paunch and prematurely thinning blond hair above a high forehead, had changed little over the past two years. The expression on his face was somewhere between grim and determined. "You are in good hands, my dear. Sir Edmund has agreed to act as your solicitor in this matter, whatever may be involved. You are to meet with him tomorrow. Until then you are to say nothing further to Scotland Yard. He believes they may attempt to prove that you were not, in fact, asleep during Alfie's murder if their other suspect falls through."

Sedgewood scowled, apparently noticing Hale for the first time. "What the hell are *you* doing here?"

"He wants to help," Sarah said.

"How—with more of his stories for the trash papers?"

It was a measure of the man that he regarded *The Morning Telegraph* and the dozens of other respectable clients of the Central Press Syndicate as "trash papers." They weren't *The Times*.

"I'm not writing anything about the case, Your Lordship. But that won't stop me from putting a bug in the ear of the man who is. Sometimes the Press can point the police in the right direction if they've gone off the rails, which I'm very much afraid they've done in this case."

The Earl regarded Hale shrewdly. "Perhaps so, perhaps not. I understand that Scotland Yard suspects that you may have had some hand in this. That hardly seems beyond imagining. You wanted to marry Sarah. I would never have permitted that, of course, but that reality did not seem to disturb your fantasies. Sarah's marriage to a thoroughly suitable partner did, however. Now that obstacle to your delusional hopes has been removed."

Charming as ever, Hale thought. Still, Hale couldn't deny his logic. It made perfect sense, objectively speaking, that Hale could have killed Alfie on his own initiative in hopes of winning Sarah back. "Fortunately, I have a witness as to my whereabouts at the time of the murder—another woman."

What was that look that Sarah gave him? Surely it couldn't be hurt or disappointment. *She* had left *him*. She must have understood that he would go on with his life without her.

"Well, that's that, then," Sedgewood said. "It's not likely that another woman would lie to protect you, given the circumstances."

"Who do you think killed Alfie?" Hale said.

The Earl shrugged. "I will leave that to the police to find out. That is what they are paid for."

"And they usually do a good job of it, more than readers of detective stories think, but not always. I believe they could use a little help on this one. Who might have wanted Alfie dead?"

"I cannot imagine unless . . . perhaps someone at the Constitutional Club, near where he died. I suppose he might have caught someone cheating at cards."

SIX
Debt and Death

"Out of debt, out of danger."
    – Thomas Fuller, *Gnomologia*, 1732

"Killed to cover up a cheating scandal?" Malone repeated over a pint that evening. Hale's working day was over. He'd spent the rest of the afternoon on interviews for the story about the lost mountaineer. But Malone's day was barely beginning. "That reminds me of the Ronald Adair murder back in the early Nineties."

Hale wrinkled his eyebrows. "That doesn't ring a bell."

"It should. That was the case that brought your friend Sherlock Holmes 'back from the dead,' as more dramatic writers than yours truly like to say."

Holmes lived still. He spent his days keeping bees at his villa on the Sussex Downs and occasionally doing a favor for old friends at Scotland Yard or his even more ancient brother in the Secret Service. But Hale hadn't seen the old man in ages.

"I seem to recall that I was in short pants at the time—and in Boston," Hale said. "Tell me about it." He motioned the bartender to bring two more pints of Fuller's London Pride to lubricate his colleague's storytelling.

"The newspapers called it the Park Lane Mystery, and quite a mystery it was. Young Adair, a handsome man about town, had been shot to death in a room locked from the inside and no weapon to be found. It turned out that Adair had caught on that his whist partner at the Bagatelle Club, Colonel Sebastian Moran, had been cheating. Even though this dishonesty had benefited him, Adair threatened to expose Moran unless the cad resigned from the club and promised to give up cards."

"And the Colonel declined rather definitively, I take it." The story was beginning to sound familiar.

Malone grabbed a fresh brew as it was deposited on the bar. "You could say that. Adair probably never knew how badly he had miscalculated. Moran was both a champion big game hunter and the chief lieutenant of the late Professor Moriarty. He shot Adair in the head through the open window of his house, using a specially built air gun. You can read all about it in *The Return of Sherlock Holmes*, the first story."

"I think I already did, but that was a long time ago. Well, if somebody killed to avoid a card cheating scandal once, it could certainly happen again. It seems to me that was one of Holmes's techniques—looking for parallel crimes in those scrapbooks of his. So maybe Sedgewood was on to something with the idea that Alfie might have caught a fellow club member cheating."

"It's not out of the question. A man who cheats at cards is no gentleman. Exposure would ruin him socially. That's plenty of motive for murder. I'll ask around whether Alfie was a card player, or hung around card players."

"Ask whom?"

"The fellow members of his clubs. I already found out that he belonged to several. And I have another little idea I want to follow up as well."

"Which is?"

"Maybe somebody owed him money. People in his set always owe each other money."

Hale nodded slowly. He remembered the Drones Club, which he had visited during the investigation of Langdale Pike's murder[3]. The members were always hitting each other up for a few quid until they got their allowance. Were all the London clubs like that? Hale didn't think so, but not being a clubbable man himself he wasn't sure.

"Or he owed money to someone else beyond his ability to pay," Hale continued Malone's thought. "Or his friends in Bloomsbury were to blame for some reason we don't know, yet."

"Or he was the victim of a random act of violence."

"Or he was a secret Fenian and Special Branch had him done in," continued Hale.

"Or he was Special Branch and the Fenians had him done in," countered Malone.

"Or a secret Egyptian society killed him as a warning to others, or, or, or!" Hale gazed into his half-finished pint. "We really are nowhere, aren't we? What are my friends at Scotland Yard up to?" Malone had just returned from an interview with Rollins.

"I'm not sure you have any friends at Scotland Yard these days," Malone said darkly. "No, that's not true. From what I hear, Chief Inspector Wiggins is four square on your side. But he's part of an old guard that's a bit on the outs just now in favor of younger blood. Commissioner Hopkins seems quite taken by the winds of change, and Dennis Rollins is as windy as they come."

---

[3] See The *Poisoned Penman*, MX Publishing, 2014.

Hale chuckled. "He's formidable, all right. I'm not so sure that his rapid climb up the ladder is entirely attributable to friends at the top. He's smart, rather devious, and a hard worker. That's why I'm not worried about being in his sights. Once he talks to Prudence Beresford, he'll realize it's time to cut his losses and look elsewhere. I just hope he gives up his notion that Sarah was involved."

"While you're hoping, you should also hope that he finds your Miss Beresford. He hasn't yet, and he's had three men working on it since this morning." Malone looked at Hale from the corner of his eye. "She does exist, doesn't she?"

"I certainly hope so." Hale drained the glass.

SEVEN
Gossip

"Foul whisperings are abroad."
— William Shakespeare, *Macbeth*, 1605

Hale had his own idea about another line of inquiry, which he kept to himself. That evening he called his fellow ex-pat friend Tom Eliot. A banker at Lloyd's, Eliot also dabbled in poetry. He even had a bit of a reputation along that line among the literati. He would know about this Bloomsbury Group.

"Yes, I am indeed well acquainted with the Woolfs," Eliot assured Hale over the telephone. "I knew that Alfie Barrington traveled in their circle." Eliot agreed to meet Hale later at The 43, an unlicensed nightclub that didn't open until midnight. Hale also wanted to talk to Aloysius Bone, who spent a good deal of his time there.

The disrespectability of The 43, a dingy little joint at 43 Gerrard Street in Soho, made it highly popular among the bright young things who had popped up now that the world was safe for democracy. Hale wouldn't be surprised to see Portia Lyme there. The owner, a rather motherly Irish woman who bribed dozens of coppers to stay in business, sat behind the cash desk of her office on the ground floor and decided who got in and who didn't. Students, soldiers, aristocracy, and journalists always got through. Hale was known there as an occasional visitor, perhaps a couple of times a year, although not a member.

"Evening, Mr. Hale," she rasped. "Who's your friend?"

"Hello, Mrs. Meyrick. You're looking lovely as always." Surprised that Eliot had never been there before, Hale made the introductions as he paid the ten-shilling non-member fee for each of them. They quickly made their way to the first-floor lounge and ordered a martini with Booth's gin for Eliot and a Manhattan for Hale.

"All I know about Bloomsbury comes from my friend Dorothy Sayers, who lives nearby," Hale said, lighting a panatela. "Tell me about this Virginia and Leonard Woolf. I just know that's she's a writer with a reputation, and not only a literary one."

"Those Woolfs don't bother with sheep's clothing." Eliot pulled a Gauloise cigarette out of the familiar blue box and lit it. "Let's see. I'll start with Virginia. Her father, Leslie Stephen, was a man of letters. She had a breakdown when he died twenty years ago. That was her second breakdown, actually—she'd also had one when her mother died."

"I don't think I need her mental history." After he said it, Hale wanted to bite his tongue. What an insensitive clod he was! Both Eliot and his English wife, Vivienne, had suffered from mental disorders.

"Right. I'll skip the other breakdowns, then." Eliot exhaled smoke from his gasper. "She married Leonard Woolf about a dozen years ago. They started Hogarth Press about five years later. Virginia sets the type herself on a hand press they bought."

"Do they publish Virginia's novels?"

Eliot picked up his martini. "Oh, yes, but more than just that. They are actually great appreciators of fine poetry." Eliot smiled at Hale's quizzical look. "Last year they came out with the first UK edition of my *Waste Land* in book form, for example."

Hale chuckled. "Okay, they run a high-quality publishing house. But tell me about Leonard."

"He's the literary editor of the *Nation*. Before that, he edited the *International Review* and the international section of the *Contemporary Review*. Several years ago, he and some of his friends founded the 1917 Club just down the street from here. It's kind of a Bohemian mirror image of a gentleman's club, and it's not restricted to gentlemen—or even to men. Very egalitarian."

"Named 1917 in honor of the Bolsheviks, I take it."

Eliot nodded. "Membership is about what you'd expect—Ramsay MacDonald, Aldous Huxley, H.G. Wells, and that sort."

"How did Woolf meet Virginia?"

"He was a friend of her brother Thorby at Cambridge."

Hale nursed his Manhattan. "What do you know about their marriage? Do they get along?" Considering the fragile state of Eliot's own union, this, too, was delicate territory, but he had to ask. Eliot didn't seem bothered.

"By all accounts they're very devoted to each other. But there is a girlfriend in the picture."

"Woolf has a girlfriend?" This was not what he'd expected.

"Not that I know of. But Virginia does. Her name is Vita Sackville-West. She's a writer and gardener married to a diplomat called Harold Nicolson."

Hale had known enough artistic types not to be shocked by that, but he quickly saw that his vague idea of Alfie being killed by Leonard Woolf out of romantic jealousy wasn't looking very likely. He expressed this thought to Eliot.

"Oh, I think both Woolfs regarded Alfie affectionately, rather as they would a puppy dog," Eliot said. "He realized he had no particular talent, but he liked to consider himself friends of those who did. And what he lacked in talent he seemed to make up for in money. Even socialists find that a useful commodity."

"Let's talk to Aloysius. He'll know who Alfie's friends and enemies were, and be more objective about it than Sarah. He's usually downstairs by this time."

Since the murder of Langdale Pike a couple of years previously, Hale's former colleague Aloysius Bone had largely succeeded in his ambition of taking Pike's place as the premier purveyor of gossip to the real trash papers, like *The Daily Megaphone*. Slight of stature, swarthy, with dark curly hair and an ingratiating manner, Bone had a way of inspiring confidences. Thus he was able to acquire information for free and sell it at good prices.

Hale and Eliot picked up their cocktails and went down to the basement, where a five-piece jazz band held forth and the dance floor was crowded. Rudolf Valentino had once been mistaken there for a waiter. Hale looked toward the tables and chairs clustered along the sides of the dance floor until he spotted Aloysius Bone sitting at what had become his "usual" table. Bone had succeeded in placing himself far enough from the band so he could hear and be heard as he traded information, and near enough to the stairs so he would see all who came and went (and who they were with).

Currently this specialist in the sleazy underbelly of journalism was talking to a pudgy, balding man that Hale recognized. His name was Hitchcock—Hitch, for short. Four years earlier, at the time of the Hangman murders, he had been a title designer at the Famous Players-Lasky moving picture studio in Islington. Hale had heard something about him becoming a director.

Hitchcock noticed Hale coming their way before Bone did. He bowed slightly in the journalist's direction. "Good evening, Mr. Hale."

"Hello, Hitch." He introduced Eliot to Hitchcock and Bone. "I must say I'm surprised to find you here."

"Are you the Hitchcock who helped write *The White Shadow?*" Eliot asked.

"Not only did he write it," interjected Bone, "he designed the sets, edited the footage, and was the assistant director."

Bone really liked to show off everything he knew, thought Hale. *I hope he is as forthcoming with what I need.*

Hale looked at Eliot. "I didn't realize you were such a film-goer."

"Not much of one, but you know how I love mysteries. This one has good and evil twins, chance meetings, a mysterious disappearance, and madness. Quite an exceptional piece of work really."

Hitch looked like he was about to burst his waistcoat buttons from the complements. "I appreciate the kind words, sir. Actually I'm just doing some research at the moment. My next film will require a scene in a seedy cabaret."

"I see." With someone else, Hale might have assumed that was just an excuse. But Hitchcock was eccentric enough that it just might be the truth. "Aloysius, I was hoping to have a word with you."

"That is very interesting," Bone said in his soft voice, "because I have something to tell you as a matter of professional courtesy. Excuse us, Hitch. Good luck with your German project."

Hitchcock bowed again and walked away. As soon as he was out of earshot, Bone said:

"I had a visit from a Scotland Yard inspector, a fellow named Rollins. He woke me up at my residence at the ungodly hour of just past noon. His manners are somewhat lacking. He asked me whether I'd seen you and the former Sarah Bridgewater together since her marriage."

"You told him no, of course."

Bone sipped a pale pink drink. "By no means, old boy. I couldn't lie to Scotland Yard, could I?"

"What?"

Eliot looked at Hale strangely.

"But you couldn't have seen me with Sarah!" Hale protested to Bone.

"I certainly did. Don't you remember? Both of you were right here at The 43 about six months go."

With a shock, Hale realized that Bone was right. He shook his head and slid into a chair at the table. He had completely forgotten—or more probably repressed the painful memory. "But I didn't bring Sarah here. I was alone. I just happened to run into her. She was with Alfie. It was all quite awkward."

"I'm sure that's true, if you say so. But I don't remember seeing Alfie that night. I just know that I saw you talking to Lady Sarah."

"That's because he was away from the table at the moment. I wasn't going to talk to her while he was there, although I really don't know why not. Our conversation was along the lines of, 'How are you?' 'I'm fine, how are you?' It was all very banal and awkward."

"Well, I didn't get close enough to hear that, although I tried. That Rollins chap seemed very interested in what I saw."

"I bet." *Damn the infernal luck.* Hale wished he had the time to wring Bone's neck. "Listen, I wanted to ask you about Alfie. I only met him once. To hear Sarah tell it, he was too loveable for anybody to want to kill him. What do you know about him?"

"Oh, he was a hail-fellow-well-met, all right—very popular because he was quite free with loaning money to his friends. He seemed to get along especially well with his brother-in-law, Charles. I've seen them here together a few times, along with Charles's fiancé and her brother. In fact, it was Sidney Lyme who told me about the dust-up Alfie got himself into last night."

"You mean with Lady Sarah?" Hale didn't know Lyme, but he was surprised that he would be sharing what was essentially family business with a professional gossipmonger.

Bone's dark, Levantine-like eyes widened. "He had an argument with her, too?"

"Never mind that. What were you talking about?"

"You can read about it tomorrow. I sold a paragraph to—" Hale had leaned forward until his nose almost touched Bone's. His *I want to know and I want to know now* look was unmistakable. "Oh, all right, Hale. He had a very loud row at the Constitutional Club last night with Howard Carter. Do you know him?"

Hale didn't know the Egyptologist, but he knew of him. The entire civilized world had heard of the man who, thanks to unfailing persistence over several years and the sponsorship of Lord Carnarvon, had discovered the treasure-laden tomb of King Tut.

EIGHT
In Search of Motive

"Whenever a man does a thoroughly stupid thing it is always from the noblest motive."
— Oscar Wilde, *The Picture of Dorian Gray*, 1891

"One suspect, known to have had a romantic relationship with Lady Sarah in the past, has been helping us with our inquiries," said Inspector Dennis Rollins of Scotland Yard, who is in charge of the investigation. "This individual has given us the name of a woman whom he says he was with at the time of the murder. After a diligent search to find this woman, however, I feel confident in saying that one Miss Prudence Beresford does not exist."

Hale threw aside the Tuesday morning edition of *The Times*, his breakfast ruined. Rollins was playing Artemis Howell, the *Times* reporter, like a violin. It was an old game: Let the suspect know he's a suspect, pour on the pressure, and then wait for him to crack like an egg and do something

stupid out of sheer panic. Careful not to mention Hale by
name, Howell had nevertheless cast suspicion on him in the
eyes of anyone who knew about his two-year relationship
with Lady Sarah—all of his friends, all of hers, and quite a
few other people that they knew more casually.

Malone would be asleep at this hour, but Hale
didn't hesitate to ring him up. His ability to sound awake
when he answered the phone impressed Hale.

"What did you find out about Alfie, Ned?"

"Couldn't you just pick up a copy of *The Morning
Telegraph* instead of disturbing my beauty sleep? I'm sure
they carried my story."

"Did you include in it everything that you found
out?"

"No, of course not. Some of it was unprintable
because of our country's benighted libel laws, and some of
it just didn't fit in."

"That's what I figured and that's why I called. Let's
trade. Give me everything you've got and I'll tell you what I
found out at The 43 last night."

"I'm not sure that I should—"

"I'm on your team, Ned. What do you think I'm
going to do with whatever you give me—tell Artie Howell
or Inspector Rollins?"

"That's a good question. What *are* you going to do
with it?"

Hale paused. "I guess that depends on what you tell
me. Look, you know my interest in this. I didn't kill Sarah's
husband and I don't think she did either. I want to make
sure that neither one of us gets railroaded into paying for a
crime we didn't commit. Something you found out may
help."

"I think you spent too much time around Sherlock
Holmes." Malone sighed. "All right, I'll give you what I've
got. Don't want to see you in the dock! I spent the evening
going around to Alfie's clubs to see if anyone would bite on

the idea that he'd spotted someone cheating. The biggest hurdle was getting into the Constitutional Club. Fortunately, my friend Challenger is a member."

"Challenger! I thought it was a *gentlemen's* club." The eccentric scientist had the physique of a grizzly bear and a temperament to match.

Malone ignored him. "But let's start with the Tankerville Club. Alfie played euchre there a couple of times a week. Everybody I talked to said that he was a cheerful loser, but probably won as much as he lost and didn't play for especially high stakes. So it's not likely that he lost a pile and looked for signs of cheating. There hasn't been a cheating scandal at the Tankerville Club since Major Prendergast was falsely accused back in the Eighties."

"Then they're overdue."

"I suppose you could say that. Nobody looked guilty when I mentioned the word 'cheating,' although I don't suppose they would. At any rate, all of Alfie's mates at the Tankerville Club thought he was absolutely the cat's whiskers, very free with paying for drinks.

"Same goes for the crowd at the Drones Club on Dover Street in Mayfair, only more so. That one's a bunch of impoverished nobility looking for wealth to marry into. I got the impression that almost everybody owed Alfie money and very few of them actually have useful employment. Several chatty gentlemen told me that the new Lord Backwater, for example, and the younger son of the Duke of Balmoral had their hands in Alfie's pockets more often than in their own."

Hale made a mental note of their names for future pursuit if the idea of a deadly debtor seemed tenable.

"The Constitutional Club is a bit more serious, generally an older membership," Malone said. "Alfie was one of the newer ones. He only joined after his marriage to Lord Sedgewood's daughter. The Earl sponsored his membership. Challenger knew him by sight, but he'd never had a conversation with him."

"Tell me about the argument."

After a pause on the other end of the line, Malone said, "What argument?"

"Alfie Barrington and Howard Carter had a very public verbal brawl at the Constitutional Club just hours before the murder."

"Damn! Nobody told me about that. Well, I guess well-bred gentlemen don't talk about things like that, at least not to members of the Press."

"That's why I have Aloysius Bone. He's neither well-bred nor a gentleman. I don't know what Alfie and Carter were fighting about, but I'm going to find out."

Hale felt a professional pride at having turned up something important that had eluded a good reporter like Ned Malone, combined with frustration that his own journalistic hands were tied. Nothing he learned would ever appear in a story under his byline, at least not until he was removed as a suspect and officially covering the case for the Central Press Syndicate. That was a journalist's nightmare.

"And there's more," he told Malone. "Alfie was in tight with a group of radical artists and writers with some unconventional habits." He filled Malone in on what he had heard about the Bloomsbury Group from Tom Eliot. "At some point I'm going to drop in on the Woolfs and see what they have to say."

"Doesn't sound too promising, bunch of free-lovers like that. What about the idea that—" Malone paused. "Well, what about the idea that Lady Sarah had a boyfriend?"

She had never really answered that question when he asked her, Hale realized. *Why not?*

"I don't know, Ned. I can only answer for myself. The last time I saw her was the day she got back to England from the trip that turned out to be her wedding voyage."

That's not true. "Wait, let me amend that. I did see her once at The 43, in a room full of other people which unfortunately included Aloysius Bone."

And Rollins is going to think I lied to him about that.

"Enoch? I hate to tell you this, but Rollins doesn't believe there is any such person as Prudence Beresford. His men can't find her."

"I know. Artie Howell dropped that little gem in *The Times* today. I presume it was in your story, too?"

"No. It seemed premature. It's only been a day."

"Does Rathbone know that you're holding back on news?"

"It was his decision."

Hale chuckled. "That old fraud! He'd be the last to admit it, but he has a soft spot."

"I wouldn't say that. I think he just has some old-fashioned ideas about fairness and justice. He'd cut you off in a heartbeat—assuming he has a heart—if he thought you'd done for Alfie. I hope you're not holding anything back about this Prudence Beresford—something that could help Scotland Yard find her."

"I told Rollins everything I know, and that's almost nothing! It's as if she existed just to give me an unprovable alibi." *It's as if . . .* "Wait a minute. Ned, what if that's just it. What if Prudence Beresford doesn't really exist at all? The whole time I was with her I felt like she had some kind of a secret. Suppose that's not her real name. Suppose she's the killer's accomplice who met me at the opera just to make sure that I didn't have a better alibi on the night of the murder. What do you think of that?"

"I think that's a brilliant idea . . . for Edgar Wallace or R. Austin Freeman. It's mystery story stuff, Enoch. Nobody would dream up something so convoluted in real life."

Malone was right, Hale thought. He was thinking like Tom Eliot or Dorothy Sayers.

"And if it's not her real name, for whatever reason," Malone added, "I don't know how you're going to find her."

Yes, how? The prospect seemed bleak. Hale strained to remember what he knew about Prudence Beresford that might be helpful. She liked opera—but opera season was over—and she liked Egypt. Egypt! The British Museum! What had she said? "Almost every Thursday I go to the North Wing of the British Museum and look at mummies and the Rosetta Stone. Needless to say, I'd rather be back in Egypt." He remembered how her face had lit up when she'd said it.

"I think I know where to find her," Hale said. "But I'll have to wait until Thursday."

She re-read the last paragraph of the *Times* story, in the grip of several emotions. How strange that the murder she had read about turned out to involve someone that she had met. And moreover, he was a suspect! But he didn't do it, poor man. He was with her at the time. The problem was, that meant that she was also with him. She couldn't come forward without Archie knowing that she'd been out with another man, however innocently. That would be most unpleasant. She was quite sure that what was good for the gander was definitely *not* good for the goose, in his view.

If Mr. Hale—Enoch—got arrested, she would have to come forward. She couldn't let an innocent man go to trial. But perhaps it wouldn't come to that.

Meanwhile, Scotland Yard was looking for her. That sentence, "Prudence Beresford does not exist" really annoyed her. *Of course she exists. Aren't one's characters real people?*

NINE
Train Talk

A wise man is never surprised.
    – Samuel Johnson, *The Rambler*, 1750

Hale spent most of Tuesday working on his story about George Leigh Mallory. Being the prime suspect in a murder case had played havoc with his concentration, but he got through it.

If the experienced mountaineer had died earlier that month on the world's highest mountain, as seemed likely, he had left behind everyone he loved: his parents, three siblings, a wife, and three children. He had also left something else, Hale suspected—an immortal quote that would be remembered long after Mallory's name was forgotten. The previous year, *The New York Times* had carried the headline **"WHY CLIMB MOUNT EVEREST?" "BECAUSE IT'S THERE," SAID MALLORY.** Whether Mallory had actually said that in so many words or the reporter had been paraphrasing was beside the point now.

Scrambling to get the story done in a day, Hale had managed to talk to Mallory's father, the Reverend Herbert

Leigh-Mallory, his younger brother, Tafford Leigh-Mallory, and his wife, Ruth. The hyphens in the last name had confused him until he found out that the father had changed the spelling about a decade before. Hale also talked to an old friend of Mallory's called Robert Graves. Mallory had taught Graves at Charterhouse School in Godalming, Surrey, and later was best man at his wedding. Graves became a poet; Mallory kept climbing mountains.

After some late-night work, Hale handed Rathbone the story on Wednesday morning as demanded.

Rathbone grunted, lit his curved pipe, and settled back to read the typed manuscript.

By Enoch Hale
Central Press Syndicate

"Because it's there."

Friends and family say those words summed up George Herbert Leigh Mallory's attitude not only to conquering mountains, but to facing other challenges in life as well.

Mallory, along with climbing partner Andrew "Sandy" Irvine, disappeared . . .

"Nice work." Rathbone said as he came to the end. He set the pages aside. "You see, a story doesn't have to be a murder mystery to be compelling." Reaching over to the credenza, Rathbone picked up a pasteboard card with the picture of a golfer on it. He flipped it at Hale. "As you know, the British Open begins tomorrow. The qualifying rounds are already underway. I want you to cover the human interest angle."

Hale took a moment to find his voice. "I've never written a sports story, sir. And I'm not much of a golfer. My handicap has more digits than my telephone number."

"How are you at mountain climbing?"

Had the old man gone daft all of a sudden? "Sir?"

"You've never climbed a mountain in your life, have you? I didn't think so. That didn't stop you from writing a fine feature story about Mallory, did it? I don't want you to write about golf, Hale, I want you to write about people. Talk to the golfers' caddies, talk to their wives and girlfriends, find the fellow who's been a professional for ten years and finally made it into the qualifying rounds of the Open and his child is sick. You know what to do."

"I do?"

The managing director glowered. "You bloody well do."

"I don't have a choice, do I?"

Rathbone consulted his pocket watch. "There's a train leaving from Euston Station in about twenty minutes and you're going to be on it. It won't get you to the Royal Liverpool Golf Club in time for the first tee-off, but soon enough. Get moving. And come back with a good story."

Hale was already on the move as he grabbed his hat. He could have sworn that out of the corner of his eye he saw his boss stifle a smile.

The cab ride to Euston gave Hale plenty of time to rue the way this day was going. He had hoped for a quick and easy assignment that would allow him to sneak in a conversation with Sidney Lyme, Charles Bridgewater's future brother-in-law. Hale wanted to know more about the argument between Alfie and Howard Carter at the Constitutional Club that Lyme had witnessed.

He made it to the station with three minutes to spare before his train departed. The trip to Liverpool would take two and a half hours, according to the schedule, and the club at Hoylake another half hour. As soon as the train was well clear of the station, he went back to the dining car for a cup of coffee. He was startled to see the familiar figure of a tall, lean man in his early forties with a high forehead.

"Plum? Is it really you?"

"None other, old boy! On my way to the British Open. Qualifying rounds, you know."

Pelham Grenville Wodehouse, "Plum" to family and friends, had been writing humorous tales of the British upper classes for two decades. Many of them were about golf, one of his passions in life. He was also well known for his stories and novels about a valet named Jeeves. Hale had interviewed Wodehouse a year ago for a story about Winston Churchill as a lark—Plum was avowedly non-political. They had run into each other once or twice since, and Plum always remembered him.

"Do you know Carter?" Plum asked, pointing to a brown-haired man with a mustache next to him. "He's a member of my favorite club."

They shook hands all round as Plum made the formal introduction of Enoch Hale, "journalist chap," and Howard Carter, "digger up of old things." Hale couldn't believe his luck. Now he would have no need to get Lyme's account of what had happened at the Constitutional Club—he would get it first-hand from the archeologist himself.

Carter should have been on Hale's list to talk to even without the argument. Carter had enjoyed the patronage of George Herbert, the Earl of Carnarvon, with whom Alfie's father-in-law had long been in competition. Hale's Central Press Syndicate colleague, the aptly named Reggie Lestrange, had written a number of stories about their unfriendly rivalry years ago, before Hale had met Sarah.

Hale recalled that Carter and Carnarvon had been in Egypt at the same time as Sarah, her father, and Alfie. The Sedgewood party had departed in September, with Sarah and Alfie marrying on the ship on their way home, but Carter had stayed in Egypt. Two months later, he had found the tomb of a relatively unknown pharaoh named Tutankhamun. The riches discovered in the previously unplundered tomb had made Carter a household name around the world.

Almost as fascinating to Hale as the mummy's tomb filled with gold and gems was Carter's amazing life story leading up to that day at the end of November 1922. Without a university degree, he had started out in Egypt as a tomb illustrator while only seventeen years old. He rose to become the first chief inspector of the Egyptian Antiquities Service. After supervising excavations in Luxor, he transferred to Lower Egypt and discovered the tombs of Thutmose I and Thutmose II, which already had been sacked by grave robbers in antiquity.

Carter resigned from the Antiquities Service in a dispute in 1905 after siding with the Egyptian site guards in a confrontation with French tourists. A kind of exile followed, during which he worked as a watercolor painter and dealer in antiquities. Then he managed to hitch on to Lord Carnarvon as his supervisor of excavations. The Earl already owned one of the most valuable collections of Egyptian artifacts in private hands, and seemed to have an insatiable desire for more.

Carter became obsessed with one tomb in particular, that of the boy pharaoh who became familiarly known as King Tut. Year after year he searched for it. By 1922, a frustrated Carnarvon served notice that this would be his last season of funding Carter. And so Carter began digging for his final season on November 1 of that year. Three days later, he found the steps that led to the tomb of Tutankhamun. He wired Carnarvon to come to Egypt for the opening of the tomb, which the latter did. When Carnarvon died the following April, the legend of King Tut's Curse was born.

Carter's biography suggested a determined and therefore disciplined man—not one who would kill another over a row in a club. Nevertheless, there was a row, if Lyme was to be believed. Maybe Carter regretted that and went to

Alfie later with the idea of making up, a gesture that ended in disaster. That seemed implausible, but not impossible.

Hale would approach the topic of Alfie Barrington slowly, he decided as they took over an empty table in the dining car—or restaurant car, as they called it on this side of the ocean.

"So—how's the mummy business?" he asked Carter jovially.

"Not so blasted good at the moment." Carter looked like he needed something stronger than coffee. "I just returned from a speaking tour in the States and a large trunk containing some important artifacts, pictures, slides, and reference material got lost along the way. I'm on my way to the Cunard docks to press them to find it."

"Hard cheese," Plum said. "But that reminds me of a very funny story."

Hale paid scant attention as the humorist went on and on with a story about losing his clubs on a golfing trip. Hale signaled the patient waiter for three cups of coffee, which were promptly delivered as Plum's tale continued.

Frustrated, Hale was trying to think of a way to bring the discussion around to Alfie Barrington. He was slowly stirring his half full cup and wondering if two hours was enough time for Wodehouse to finish the story when his opportunity came. Plum ended with, "Well, anyway, it's good to see you, Carter. It's been ages. Sorry I missed you at the Constitutional the other night. Heard you were there."

Perfect! Good old Plum had introduced the subject for him.

Carter grunted. "Not my warmest welcome home!"

Hale waited for him to elaborate. When he didn't, Hale said, "I heard there was some kind of a row involving Alfred Barrington, the man who was stabbed outside the club later that night."

Carter looked as if he'd been slapped. "Where the devil did you hear that?"

"I happen to know a chap named Sidney Lyme." That was only a slight exaggeration. They *had* met. "He's a member of the Constitutional and he overheard the argument."

"Oh, Lyme." The expression on Carter's face was as if he'd just bit into a particularly sour lime. "He used to knock about Egypt a bit. Knowing him, he must have told you that I was the other fellow. I feel bad that Barrington's dead, but that doesn't change that fact that he was a fool and a rotter."

Hale slowly lit a panatela. He had to be careful not to overplay his hand. "I can't say I was a fan of Alfie Barrington myself. Fact is, the cad stole my girl and married her."

Carter gave Hale a sympathetic look. "They didn't seem a very happy couple, if that makes you feel any better. From what I gathered, they'd had an argument that night. He came to the club and started hitting the bottle rather hard. If he hadn't been drunk he probably wouldn't have insulted me."

"But he was such an inoffensive chap!" Plum protested.

"Not to me!" Carter looked around and, seeing the waiter, signed for more coffee before he continued. "Barrington adopted his father-in-law's rivalry with Lord Carnarvon as if it were his own. With His Lordship's untimely death, that rivalry was transferred to me. I'll give you an example. I was in a dispute with the Egyptian government when I left there in March for my speaking tour. The Egyptians wanted me to use Tutankhamun's tomb as something of a tourist attraction, which was interfering with my work. But when I allowed some of the expedition members' wives into the tomb, my former friends at the Egyptian Antiquities Service demanded the keys to the tomb. Well, I couldn't have that. So I locked the gates and took the keys with me. The Egyptian government took over the site by force. Barrington seized on this bother as a wedge to try to get the Antiquities Service to give the tomb of Tutankhamun over to Lord Sedgewood's man, Linwood Baines, and keep me out. It didn't work, but it was a near thing."

Hale waited as the waiter poured more coffee.

"Is that what you were fighting about on Sunday night?" Hale asked once the man had left.

"Well, I could hardly ignore the issue when I saw him at the club, could I?"

"But you said he insulted you."

Carter nodded. "I'm very much a self-made man, gentlemen. Despite my record of over thirty-three years in Egypt, Barrington attacked my credentials because I don't have a blasted university education. I told him that I've never made any secret of that, and that he ought to take a hard look closer to home if that sort of thing is so important to Lord Sedgewood."

"Meaning what?"

"Meaning Baines, my counterpart in the Sedgewood camp. He claims to be an Oxford man, but I've heard that isn't true. He may well be a fraud, a charlatan!"

Hale sat stunned for a moment at the vehemence in Carter's voice.

"You don't suppose," interjected Plum, "that Barrington could have confronted this Baines chap, do you?"

TEN
An Old Friend

The perfect friendship is that between good men, alike in their virtue.

— Aristotle, *The Nicomachean Ethics*, 340 B.C.

"I can't believe that Hale would have done it," Chief Inspector Wiggins said, putting down his pint of Guinness with an emphatic thump. "He couldn't have."

Sherlock Holmes, sitting across the table at the Northumberland Arms, raised a grey eyebrow. "Couldn't have killed the man who married the woman he loved?" Holmes sipped his whiskey and soda. "Men have murdered for far less reason. Most men are not the thinking creatures that we like to believe them to be. You, of all people, should know that. How many homicides have you investigated over the years? They are as common in the drawing room as in the gutter."

"Oh, he might have killed the blighter, but he would have owned up to it. He's a man and no mistake about it. But Rollins won't see that. All Rollins will see is a chance for a clever headline and his name on the promotion list." Wiggins leaned his chair back on two legs and waived his arm out in front of him punctuating each word he said with a thrust of his hand, "Reporter Writes Own Death Warrant." The chair dropped back to the floor with a crack. "Or some such catchy phrase. Rollins, bother!"

Holmes smiled. "You remind me of the way Lestrade and Gregson treated my 'clever theories,' as they liked to say." Wiggins would remember them well, two stalwarts of the Yard back when he had been the leader of Holmes's irregular force of street Arabs.

"Rollins is no Sherlock Holmes. He's hard working, ambitious, and not at all short on brains. I'll give him all that. But"—Wiggins put a finger to his nose—"he can't smell the truth. He isn't able to sort, if you know what I mean. He can't tell the difference between the significant and the trivial. He confuses them all the time and I have a feeling we have more than one innocent man in jail 'cause he can't tell the difference. He's a bit low on street smarts."

There was no lacking that in Wiggins, Holmes thought. He had grown up on the streets, picking up coins from Sherlock Holmes for directing his little band of urchins to find a taxicab or a steam launch. And the lad Wiggins had been smart enough to know that there was no future in the streets picking up those coins. The future was in working hard and taking opportunities as they came.

"Why are you telling me this, Wiggins?"

"I was hoping you'd want to help Hale, seeing as how you worked together on that Hangman business and the Pike murder."

Holmes thought for a moment as he gently rotated the glass on the tablecloth. "I'm afraid he hasn't asked for my help, Wiggins."

"That's a matter of pride I suppose. Or, maybe he's waiting for you to offer."

Or maybe he just forgot about me, Holmes thought. *Maybe everyone has forgotten about me. I'm seventy years old and I look it. I've been officially retired more than twenty years—not that Mycroft didn't put me to work anyway, especially during the Great*

War. It's even been seven years since Watson has published one of his highly romanticized accounts. My gait is slower now and I don't remember things as well as I used to. If Hale asked me to help, could I even do it?

Holmes stood up. As he did, Wiggins realized that his old mentor now looked the part of an older man. His clothes were somewhat dated and they hung a little loosely. His eyes were still bright, his wit still quick, but yes, the hair was grey and the movements not as spry as he remembered.

Wiggins smiled to himself and looked at his own attire—not quite as loose at it should be—and he knew the hairline was staring to recede. The sedentary life behind the desk of a chief-inspector was taking its own toll.

"It's always good to see you, Wiggins," Holmes said. "Thank you for calling. But I think that I had best get back to my bees."

"Then you won't help, Mr. Holmes?" The look of disappointment on Wiggins's face was plain.

Holmes hesitated a moment, then placed a hand on his old friend's shoulder.

"Should Hale call for assistance I will do what I can, but perhaps my time has passed. Good day, old friend."

ELEVEN
An Awkward Surprise

In matters of love a woman's oath is no more to be minded than a man's.
— John Vanbrugh, *The Relapse*, 1696

Within a few hours at the Royal Liverpool Golf Club, Hale had talked to a dozen duffers, hangers-on, and golfers' wives—quite enough for the light feature that Rathbone was looking for. The American who was playing, Walter Hagen, had won the 1922 Open. And one Scot by the name of MacIver was having none of that as a possible repeat. The old gentleman had literally followed Hale around for the better part of an hour giving his personal discourse on the game and the inherent right of a Britisher to win it (preferably a Scot). Hale allowed as how Hagen was three strokes back today and the Empire should have nothing to worry about. *A £75 prize seems hardly worth crossing the Atlantic for*, thought Hale as he made his escape from McIver. He was glad he was only a Saturday duffer.

The return trip to London by the 9.04 into Euston Station gave him the chance to organize his notes for writing, with plenty of time left over for pondering what Howard Carter had said. He sat back in the carriage and tried to think about it logically, as Sherlock Holmes would.

He even thought of calling Holmes, but that didn't seem right. Didn't the old man deserve his peace? Besides, Hale should have learned a thing or two from the world's greatest consulting detective. He just needed to put his mind to it. All right, then.

If Linwood Baines was a poseur who had lied about his background in order to get Lord Sedgewood to fund his expeditions—and to line his pockets—that might be a secret worth killing for. But in that case, why not also kill Carter—and whoever told him? They all knew the secret. But perhaps killing Alfie wasn't a rational act. Suppose Alfie confronted Baines and he reacted like a cornered animal. But Alfie was killed right outside the Constitutional Club just hours after his encounter with Carter. What were the chances that he would have had the opportunity to challenge Baines so soon after Carter suggested that something was amiss? Well, maybe Alfie just happened to have had an appointment with Baines that night, to talk about a loan or something. Stranger things had happened.

Hale was still bouncing ideas around like that—raising objections to Baines's guilt and then knocking them down—when he returned to the headquarters of the Central Press Syndicate on Fleet Street. A familiar form, heart-achingly familiar, stood in the shadow of the doorway. Her hair was covered by a dark blue draped crown hat and her dress by a mid-calf length coat in what the latest fashion magazines called a grackle head blue. She looked even more tired than when he had seen her on Monday. Hale wondered when she had last slept.

"Sadie—" *Damn it, where did that come from?* Sadie was the name under which he had first known her—not as the daughter of a peer, but as a music hall singer. "I mean, Lady

Sarah, what are you doing here?" *Keep it polite, formal, unemotional.*

"Can we talk? In private, I mean."

Hale looked around, half afraid to see Rollins watching from across the street. "Come inside."

Hale didn't have an office of his own. He took Sarah past the mass of desks in the pit to the conference room near the back door, followed by the appreciative gaze of Ned Malone. This was totally inappropriate, being behind a closed door with a recently widowed woman, but Hale didn't give a damn.

"What's happened?" he asked as he closed the door and took a seat opposite Sarah.

"I saw Father today for the first time since I left his townhouse yesterday morning. Charles and I had dined with him on Monday, and I stayed overnight because I didn't want to go back to Bedford Place. Father told me this afternoon that policeman, Inspector Rollins, showed up after I left yesterday and interrogated him about the murder weapon."

"I don't understand. Why would Rollins ask the Earl about that?"

Sarah leaned over and grabbed Hale's hand as if she were clutching a lifeline. "Rollins said an informer called and told him that a dagger from the funerary equipment of Queen Ahhotep, mother of Ahmosis I of the 18th Dynasty, was used to kill Alfie—a dagger from Father's collection. He demanded to see it."

Hale didn't know what to make of that. It was coming at him too fast. "What did your father say?"

"He denied owning such an item. Oh, Enoch, what if Inspector Rollins can prove that he was lying?"

"How can he do that? Unless . . . do you mean he *was* lying?"

She sighed. "Father couldn't admit to owning the dagger because he acquired it by, let's say, less than legal means. Queen Ahhotep's tomb had two similar daggers—one of solid gold, both dagger and sheath, which was reported to the Egyptian authorities, and the one that Father managed to get, which has a copper blade with gold handle and gold sheath. Father kept it with the rest of his collection in the library."

"Who told Rollins about it?"

"He said the call was anonymous, although he made it clear he wouldn't have told me if he'd known."

"Who do you think it was?"

"One of the servants, I suppose."

"Does Rollins suspect your father?"

Sarah shook her head. "Oh, no. He still suspects me"—there was the slightest hesitation—"and you. He thinks the dagger does exist, and that I took it while I was visiting Father, and that Father is covering up for me." Her voice trembled, on the verge of tears. "He said I could have taken it out of the library in my handbag, and there is no denying that is true. It's my favorite room in the house and I always spend a lot of time there. If it were the murder weapon, could Scotland Yard prove it?"

"I should think they could match the wounds to the weapon, but it would be difficult to say it was an exact match." Hale scooted his chair over and put his arm around her in a brotherly way. "Buck up. If worse comes to worse, your father can produce the dagger and prove that it didn't kill Alfie. I'm sure he'd do that to save you from the dock."

"But he can't."

"Why not?"

"Because Father doesn't have the dagger, Enoch." She hesitated. "It's . . . it's . . . been stolen. Oh, this is all such a mess!"

Hale unconsciously tightened his grip on Sarah. "The theft of the dagger—it just happened recently?"

"Yes." Again she hesitated. "When Father looked for it after Rollins left, it wasn't there."

That couldn't be a coincidence—but it could be a cover-up, a story that Sedgewood told his daughter to hide the fact that he had gotten rid of the weapon used to kill her husband. Having been illegally taken out of Egypt, there would be no record of it being in his possession. If Sedgewood hadn't shown it around, then the only people in England who could testify to the dagger's existence were Sarah, who would lie to defend her father; her brother, Charles; and perhaps some servants who wouldn't dare to accuse a peer—or would they? Hale still didn't get the whole British class thing.

All this was too much to spell out to Sarah. He simply said, "Maybe Rollins *should* suspect your father."

She moved away from Hale. "How could you! I thought you wanted to help."

"I do want to help . . . you. I know you didn't kill Alfie. Your father I'm not so sure about."

"You're being terribly unfair just because you and Father never got along."

"I got along fine. *He* was the problem."

She ignored that. "Father always liked Alfie very much; you know that. Our marriage pleased him—more than it pleased me, if the truth be told. He had no reason in the world to kill Alfie."

"Your brother said the Earl was upset about Alfie's relationship with the Woolfs and their Bloomsbury Group."

"Upset, yes. Homicidal, no."

But Hale saw something in her wide green eyes that made him wonder whether she believed what she was saying.

"Did your father send you to talk to me?"

"Good heavens, no! He'd be horrified and furious if he knew that I was asking your help!"

"How much help can I be when Rollins thinks that you and I were in it together?"

"Oh, Enoch!" Her eyes filled with tears. He held her close again.

"I'm not completely out of it," he said, hoping to encourage her. "I've been asking some questions. I have a few for you, too. Will you promise to answer me honestly, even if my questions are uncomfortable?"

"Of course. I know that you are my friend and want only the best for me."

That hurt, though he tried not to show it. What man who wants to be a woman's husband is happy to be called her friend? He steeled himself to be hurt much more.

"That argument you had with Alfie the night that he died—was it about another man?"

She paused. "Yes and no. I guess I'd better start by saying that I realized before the ship had even docked that I'd been a fool to marry Alfie. It was all wrong, wrong, wrong."

"You didn't love him?"

"Oh, but I did! I loved him exactly like I love Charles, as a sister loves a brother. Marrying him was the biggest mistake of my life. But I knew it was a mistake I had to live with. Divorce was unthinkable. I couldn't do that to Alfie. He was such a dear—and such a bore. I actually rather liked it that he hung around with people much more interesting than he was, those Bloomsbury people."

"Did Alfie know how you felt?"

"He never said so, and I tried hard to be a good wife. But a woman can't hide her feelings. I think that's why he spent so much time away from home. Charles was the only one who knew how unhappy I had been. I had to confide in someone. He, at least, understood both wanting to please Daddy and fearing the loss of his love and help at the same time. After all," she smiled sideways at Enoch, "he had been through much the same thing."

"And what happened the night of the argument? What was it about?" That's what he had been building up to.

"Alfie was jealous of a photograph that he found in my bag. I don't know how he came to be looking in there. Maybe he guessed that there was such a photograph. At any rate, that's what he found—a picture of the man I realize now is the only man I have ever loved."

She reached into the silk-lined depths of her black dress bag and pulled out the photo. With a shy look on her pretty face, she handed it to Hale.

Hale recognized it right away. The picture was in a cellulite envelope, like those used by stamp collectors. It showed no wear and had been carefully taken care of, probably only recently added back to her purse. The image showed Sarah at Murray's Night Club. The man next to her, with his hand on hers, was a slightly younger Enoch Hale.

TWELVE
Finding the Alibi

"If this were played upon a stage now, I could condemn it as an improbable fiction."
— William Shakespeare, *Twelfth Night*, 1601

Hale remembered when the photo had been taken, one night when they were out with Tom Eliot shortly after the Hangman Murders were solved.

He could feel his neck turning red.

"You sure had a unique way of showing your love," he said. "You married another guy."

Sarah winced. "I was worse than a fool, Enoch; I was a romantic fool. We were in Egypt. Alfie seemed every bit the intrepid amateur archeologist. The excavation season hadn't even begun yet and Alfie had never picked up a trowel in his life, but somehow that didn't matter. When he proposed under the stars in the Valley of the Kings, it seemed so romantic that I just didn't know how to say no."

"If you'd sent me a wire, I could have told you how."

As soon as the words were out of his mouth, Hale wished that he could take them back. Sarah flinched as though he'd slapped her, and he hadn't intended that. He shook his head, shrugged his shoulders, and moved on.

"Rollins said you told him the maid must have heard wrong. Why did you lie?"

"Don't you see, Enoch?" Her voice was pleading. "I didn't want you brought into this. I didn't realize that you would be anyway, just because of what we once were to each other."

And could be again? Was that what she was trying to imply?

Hale stood and walked around the conference table trying to gather his thoughts. He needed to concentrate on the issue at hand. On balance, he didn't like it that she lied to Rollins. Her reason sounded good, but if she lied to Scotland Yard she could lie to a Yankee reporter who had been head over heels in love with her. *And still was?* Hale wasn't sure, and this was no time to try to work it out. However he felt about Sarah, she could be lying about the argument with Alfie. Maybe it was about another man and she didn't want Hale to know about him any more than she wanted Rollins to.

"I'm so thankful you have an alibi," Sarah added.

"Yes, I was at a performance of *Aida* at Covent Garden. The woman I was with can attest to that." Sarah looked hurt, as though he had betrayed her—which was ridiculous. She was the one who had married before he'd had a chance to propose. What did she care how he spent his Sunday evening? But then, she had once been an actress of a sort. If she wanted to gain his sympathy, it would come naturally to her to appear hurt that he'd been with another woman that day.

"Unfortunately," he added, "I don't know who the woman is."

The next day, the day the Open began, found Hale at the British Museum when he was supposed to be back at the Royal Liverpool Golf Club for another feature story. Since Rollins and his men still hadn't found her, he was convinced that "Prudence Beresford" had been a false name dreamed up by a bored wife in search of adventure and romance. And yet . . . her flirting—and there was some flirting—had been quite tentative, which didn't seem to fit. But that mystery could wait. First he had to find her. He had just one hope. If it didn't work out, he would be forced to place an advert in the newspaper agony columns.

Unless she had been lying to him, Thursday was the day she often went to the world-famous museum, just two blocks from Sarah's home on Bedford Place. Sherlock Holmes had also once lived near the British Museum, in rooms on Montague Street, in his early days as a consulting detective with few clients. Holmes! Hale should have called the old man days ago, retirement and those infernal bees of his be damned.

Based on the collections of Sir Hans Sloan, the vast, temple-shaped Museum was like the attic of the Empire in terms of the depth and diversity of what was to be found there. But "Prudence" had mentioned the Rosetta Stone, that ancient Egyptian stele inscribed with the same message in hieroglyphs, Demotic, and ancient Greek. It had been on display at the Museum since 1802, just three years after its discovery by a soldier with Napoleon's expedition to Egypt.

Hale stood in front of it, wishing that it held the key to Alfie Barrington's murder as it had held the key to Egyptian hieroglyphics. He went back to his wild idea that "Prudence" had been part of a plot to frame Sarah—and him. Who would do such a thing? *Cui bono?* The real killer, obviously, would benefit by throwing the suspicion on someone else, but why them? There had to be a reason to frame them in particular. If Sarah were convicted of Alfie's murder, she couldn't inherit his money. Where would it go then?

It's always startling, and at first almost unbelievable, to see in the flesh a person you've been thinking of. So that was Hale's first reaction when he realized, after half an hour or so in front of the granite-like rock, that the woman standing a few feet to the right of him, with a few other gawkers in between them, was "Prudence Beresford."

Moving slowly, he stepped back from the Rosetta Stone and approached her from her left.

"Hello, Prudence," he whispered in her ear, dripping sarcasm on the name.

Curiously, she didn't seem surprised.

"I knew I shouldn't have come today," she said, resignation in her voice. "I was fairly sure I mentioned my Thursday habit to you, and of course you would remember that. You're no Captain Hastings, Mr. Hale. You're no fool."

He didn't know who she was talking about, and he didn't care. "That remains to be seen. Listen, I'm in a spot of trouble and I need your help."

"I know. I read about it in *The Times*. Scotland Yard is looking for me." She started walking slowly away, with a nod to indicate that he should follow. Walking through the vast halls of the museum, they could avoid other people and make sure they weren't overheard.

"If you know that, why didn't you come forward?" *Unless that was part of the plan.*

"I'm afraid that doing so would put me in an embarrassing position that I wish to avoid. That's very selfish of me, no doubt, but there it is."

Hale felt his pulse rising. "My situation is a little more serious. A Scotland Yard inspector gives every indication of wanting to measure me for a hangman's noose. As I happen to be fond of my own neck, this makes me uncomfortable. Look, I need an alibi, and you're it. All you would have to do is tell the truth. Surely even Rollins wouldn't believe that a woman would lie to protect a man who killed another man to be with his wife."

She looked at him strangely.

"Don't ask me to say that again," he said, "because I'm not sure that I could."

"I understand your point. Complex plots are nothing new to me." She paused in front of a black statue of the Egyptian god Horus. "Let me tell you about my circumstances. First of all, I am married."

"That is not exactly a news flash," Hale said dryly. "As you said, I'm no fool."

"You surprise me. I didn't think you were the sort of man who would keep company with a married woman."

She sounded disappointed in him. How did that figure? She was the one who was married, she had asked him to meet her at the opera, and now she was moralizing. *Women!*

"I'm willing to stipulate that if Rollins put me in the dock on charges of not being a saint, he could probably get a conviction," Hale said. "But I never thought about you being married until the second time, at *Aida*. It just never occurred to me. When I looked for a wedding ring, you weren't wearing one, although it looked like you had. Now, I don't know a lot about marriage, having never been married, but I'm going to guess that when a woman takes off her wedding ring and meets a man she barely knows for a night at the opera, her relationship with her husband is not the best."

She nodded. "I suppose it's an old story. We married on Christmas Eve, 1914. He was home on leave from the war. By then it was clear that this wasn't going to be the short war we had all expected at the beginning, home by Christmas and all that. But he had a 'good war'—no injuries—and I made myself useful here at home as a volunteer nurse and dispenser.

"Archie left the army in 1919 and went into finance. Things were all right for a while. Last year we had a marvelous adventure traveling the world for months to promote the British Empire Exhibition. But I missed our daughter terribly, and when we came home last October Archie had no job. I don't think he liked it that we got by on my inheritance from my father and the money I make from writing. Earlier this year Archie got a job and I made enough from selling serial rights to buy my dear bottle-nosed Morris Cowley."

"So what's the problem?"

"If only I knew! It seems that nothing I say or do is right. I'm too cheerful! I'm too gloomy! That's why I came alone to the opera, but it was nice to have an intelligent person to talk to before and after. You see, I've had to find ways to amuse myself that don't involve Archie. He spends all of his weekends on golf. We used to golf together but now he won't let me play with him because he says I'm not good enough. Do you play golf?"

"I know how to hold a club." *And I'm supposed to be at the British Open right now, earning my paycheck.* "What you're telling me is that things aren't good with your husband, but you don't want to make it worse."

"I still have hopes, Mr. Hale. And a daughter."

This woman's marriage was hanging by a thread. Hale couldn't bring himself to cut it off. He sighed. "Without you swearing to Scotland Yard that I was with you on Sunday night, I have no alibi. I'll just have to find another way out of this pickle."

"What do you mean?"

"I'll solve the murder myself, like an amateur sleuth in one of those damned detective novels. I've been involved in something of the sort before."

The woman next to him colored. "Now you're making fun of me, Mr. Hale."

"What do you mean?"

"Don't play the coy American with me."

Hale was losing his patience. "Listen, Mrs. Whoever You Are, I have no idea what you're talking about."

"Do you seriously mean you don't know who I am?"

Hale rubbed his mustache. "You mean Prudence Beresford isn't your real name?" Now he *was* joking.

"I'm sorry. How silly of me—I had thought I had completely given myself away by my choice of a pseudonym, but I suppose you are not familiar with my work. Why would you be? I write those damned detective novels, Enoch. My name is Agatha Christie."

THIRTEEN
Looking for an Introduction

Honest, unaffected distrust of the powers of man is the
surest sign of intelligence.
                    – G.C. Lichtenberg, *Reflections*, 1799

"Christie!" Tom Eliot exploded. "I should have
known."

Hale regarded him skeptically across Eliot's desk at
Lloyds. "How so?"

"You know how I love detective stories." Eliot ran
his hand through his hair while he shook his head. "I've
read all of her books—*The Mysterious Affair at Styles*, *The
Secret Adversary*, *Murder on the Links*, and *Poirot Investigates*. Her
second one, *The Secret Adversary*, is about a bright young
couple named Tommy and Tuppence. But Tuppence's real
name is Prudence, and at the end of the story she marries
Tommy, whose last name is Beresford."

"So she adopted a name she'd already made up for
one of her characters?" Hale said. "That's not very
imaginative."

"Fooled you, old boy. Besides, Mrs. Christie has
quite an imagination, I assure you—international intrigue

and all that. And I think she's on to something with that little Belgian detective of hers."

On this Friday morning, Hale was supposed to be at the last day of the British Open, working on a final feature story. Rathbone would never know that he wasn't. Yesterday, arriving late in Hoylake after his conversation with Agatha Christie, he had had the good fortune to run into a reporter acquaintance named Willie Gordon.

"What are you doing here?" Hale had asked. "Golf is a bit out of your line, isn't it?" Gordon, a round man with a fringe of white hair, covered politics for *The Morning Star*.

"I'm on the sick," Gordon explained in a near whisper.

"You don't look sick."

Gordon winced. "Be a mate, will you? Forget you saw me. Pillsbury would have my hide."

So that was it! Old Gordon was malingering so he could watch some golf and his notoriously foul-tempered editor had better not get wind of it.

"Willie, how would you like to do me a return favour and earn a few extra pounds in the process?"

Gordon had quickly accepted Hale's offer to pay him handsomely for conducting interviews and giving Hale the notes. Thus Hale was able to turn in an acceptable piece of work even though he had arrived very late on the scene. He actually did do the writing, he told his conscience; it was only most of the quotes that the veteran reporter had supplied. The scheme had worked so well that Hale had hired Gordon for an encore the next day, freeing Hale up to pursue some possibilities in Alfie's murder that he was certain Rollins wouldn't touch.

"You told me all about the Woolfs," he said to Eliot. "Can you introduce me to them? It's time I asked them some questions."

"Nothing simpler. Let's go round to the 1917 Club."

"Will they let us in?"

"They'll let anybody in, with the possible exception of a capitalist."

Hale had never been to the 1917 Club, but it was just a few doors down from The 43 on Gerrard Street in Soho. The building itself was a rather unimposing four-story on a corner lot. The green door at the entrance was flanked by an old pair of sconces that seemed rather dated. In fact the whole inside of the "club" had more the appearance of a flat ready to let than a meeting place for the socialist elite. Hale looked around to see if he recognized anyone.

"Isn't that man with the moustache H.G. Wells?" he asked Eliot.

"No, I believe his name is Blevins. He's some sort of minor government functionary."

"Oh."

"I don't see . . . Oh, there's Virginia."

She was a tall, lean, angular, and rather nervous-looking woman with long hair gathered in back.

Eliot was just completing his introduction of Hale when her long-faced husband joined them with a "Hello, Eliot" that sounded more lugubrious than jaunty.

As previously agreed upon, Eliot explained to the literary couple that his old friend Hale was in a bit of a spot.

"It seems that Scotland Yard is casting a wary eye on him because he was once romantically involved with the lovely Mrs. Barrington, and more power to him for that."

"Alas, poor Alfie," Virginia said. "I knew him, Eliot."

"Harmless sort of fellow, one would think," her husband put in.

"Then you don't have any idea who would have wanted to kill him?"

"Good heavens, no!" Leonard Woolf's equine face registered shock, or a good imitation of it. "I heard he'd been stabbed to death, but I didn't catch the details. I assumed it was a robbery or something of that sort."

Hale shook his head. "It definitely wasn't a robbery. His money was still in his pockets and his watch wasn't touched."

"Alfie was pathetically eager to please," Virginia said. "That tended to annoy one, but surely not to the point of murder."

"He spent a lot of time with you and your friends, didn't he?" Hale asked, knowing the answer from his conversation with Sarah and Charles.

"I'm afraid so," Leonard said.

"I've heard that Lord Sedgewood wasn't happy about that."

"The whole bloody clan was a bit nose up in the air about it," Virginia said, "even that brother-in-law, Charles. He was another stuffed shirt."

"And he was quite the heavy partier himself when he came back from the War, or so Alfie said," her husband added. "Apparently his father cut him off from his allowance until he changed his ways to get back into the old boy's good graces. Capitalist money will do that."

That's one way of looking at it, Hale thought, although Sedgewood was hardly an old boy—barely a decade older than the Woolfs.

"This is all rather unpleasant sort of talk," Eliot said. "Can't someone say something nice about the poor bastard who's dead?"

"Well, he was free with his ill-gotten family funds," Leonard said, "always willing to loan his friends money, sometimes rather large amounts."

Bone had said the same, and Ned Malone had suggested that maybe somebody had decided to shove a knife into Alfie rather than pay him back.

"You wouldn't happen to know who the recipients of this largesse were?" Hale asked.

Leonard appeared to think about it. "I don't know that I ever heard. It was just common talk that Alfie was an easy touch."

Hale was not at all sure that Leonard was being quite honest in his statement. Something in the look he had given Virginia made Hale think he knew something he didn't want to share. A moment's uneasy silence followed.

Virginia looked as if she had made a decision when she turned away from Leonard and spoke again to Hale.

"I bet Charles hit him up," Virginia said. "His father probably keeps him on a tight leash financially. And I would suspect that Alfie's friend Baines, the archaeologist fellow, was into his pockets as well. Alfie brought both of them around now and then. Charles was tedious but quite comfortable with our views on the late war. He was one of the millions who had suffered for the stupidity of the generals." She took a long breath before she continued. "Baines had even less to recommend him. He was a name-dropper and quite impressed with himself."

FOURTEEN
Baines

Time and Chance reveal all secrets.
  – Mary De La Riviere Manley, *The New Atlantis*,
  1709

Linwood Baines lived two doors down from the Egyptian consulate, which was located at 26 South Street. The building had the same external look as the one on either side of it, obviously built as part of a row development. Stone covered the face of the ground floor and the upper levels were red brick. The only thing distinctive about this particular house was the covered porch, which extended out from the face of the building, and a spiked iron railing, which circumscribed the six steps to the door and the concrete yard that lay between the house and the sidewalk. Hale suspected that Baines was trying to ingratiate himself with the neighboring Aziz Pasha Ezzat, Minister Plenipotentiary to the Court of St. James.

Virginia Woolf had been the second person to mention Baines as a possible suspect in Alfie's killing, although for different reasons. Two days earlier, Howard Carter had claimed that Baines had been lying about his credentials as an archeologist. It was past time for Hale to check him out.

He had called ahead, so Baines was expecting him. The door opened before Hale could knock. An elderly gentleman emerged and strolled past Hale with a quick nod in his direction as he passed. He was a stout individual, like an athlete past his prime, and wore a thick grey mustache.

Baines, about forty years old with strawberry blond hair and the crooked nose of a boxer or street fighter, stood in the open doorway. Hale sized up his perfectly tailored grey suit as Saville Row. *He spends a lot on clothing*, Hale thought, *but he shows his visitor to the door himself. That means he doesn't have a servant. Maybe he's hard up for money. Maybe he owed a lot to Alfie and couldn't pay him back.*

Baines watched the guest depart for a few moments before turning his attention to the newcomer. "Mr. Hale?"

"Right."

The formalities of handshaking accomplished, they entered the house together.

"Looks like you're having a busy morning," Hale commented.

"Oh, it's just the usual thing. That was a collector of antiquities who just left, a fellow named Burton Hill. Came here to get my advice on a purchase, but couldn't help talking about Alfie's murder. I suppose that's going to be the order of the day. Well, come in, sir."

He spoke with machine-gun rapidity and an open manner. Hale was going to find it hard not to like him.

With no servants in evidence, just as Hale had expected, Baines offered him tea from a sideboard in the sitting room. As Hale added sugar, Baines said, "I know about you."

Hale froze for a second, and then stirred his tea. "What is it that you know about me, Mr. Baines?"

Baines sat back, teacup in hand. "You said on the phone that you're a friend of the Bridgewater family and that you're trying to help Lady Sarah. I daresay you are a friend to some in the family and not to others. Lady Sarah has mentioned your name many times in my presence, and always with a great deal of affection. I believe she regrets that . . . well, let's just say she's certainly quite fond of you."

Hale sipped tea, using the cup to hide the smile of satisfaction on his face.

"I gather, then, that you know Lady Sarah rather well."

"One could say that. I've spent a lot of time around her and Mr. Barrington because of my relationship with His Lordship."

"Are you aware that Scotland Yard suspects she may have had something to do with her husband's death?"

Baines snorted. "Preposterous! Lady Sarah would hesitate to kill a scorpion that was about to strike her. Someone else would have to do it for her. She certainly wouldn't kill anyone."

Hale sat forward. "Now that's interesting."

"What?"

"I would have expected you to say that she couldn't have killed Mr. Barrington because she was very devoted to him."

"Devoted?" Baines appeared to consider the word. "That depends on what one means by the word. Lady Sarah was a dutiful wife to Mr. Barrington, certainly, from what I could observe. I didn't get the sense, however, that theirs was a love match. Forgive me, Mr. Hale, I see that I've shocked you." *No, you have delighted me, Baines.* "I've overstepped my bounds. You will write me down as a hopeless gossip."

Hale's heart soared. Although Sarah had essentially told Hale the same thing, Baines's comment was a third-party confirmation of her story. That meant that Sarah hadn't just been telling him what she must certainly know he would want to hear.

"I hope you didn't tell Inspector Rollins that," Hale said. "It wouldn't do Sarah a bit of good."

The archeologist's jaw dropped. "Inspector? You mean Scotland Yard? The police haven't talked with me. Do you think they will?"

"Perhaps not. I'm poking into different corners than they are. For example, did you owe Alfie money?"

"Certainly not! What makes you ask that?"

"I understand that a lot of his friends owed him money."

"Yes, but I wasn't in the category of friend."

"You didn't get along?"

Baines set down his teacup with a clink. "That's not what I meant. Mr. Barrington was my sponsor's son-in-law. We weren't on the same social level, and thus we didn't quite play bridge together." He spoke dryly, stating the obvious with a light touch that said he was resigned to his station in life.

Hale believed him. The nature of his relationship with Alfie would be too easily checked to lie about. Besides, the card game that Alfie played with his pals was euchre.

"Why do you ask?"

"A friend of mine has a bee in his bonnet that maybe somebody killed Alfie to avoid paying back a loan."

"And you think that I—"

"I don't think anything. I'm just asking questions and collecting information. That's what reporters do. The only difference is, I'm not doing this for the Central Press Syndicate—at least, not at this point. As I said on the telephone, I'm just trying to find out something that might help Sarah." *And myself.*

"Well, at any rate, I don't think it's very likely that one of Mr. Barrington's perennially hard-up friends would go so far as to kill him to avoid debt service," Baines said. "They haven't the energy. Besides, Mr. Barrington would more likely have lent them the money to make the payment! It would be interesting to know how much he ever actually recouped from his loans." Baines sat back in his chair. His eyes played about the room and he was clearly lost in thought for a moment. Hale left the silence hanging and waited for the next comment. He noticed that Baines's eyes came to rest on some Egyptian curios on the fireplace mantle. "No, Mr. Hale," Baines finally continued in a voice barely audible, "you ought to take a hard look at Howard Carter."

Hale braced himself to hear Baines's version of the argument between Alfie and Carter at the Constitutional Club on Sunday night, but that's not what Baines had in mind.

"There was bad blood between Carter and Lord Sedgewood. I've thought for a long time that Carter would kill His Lordship if he had the chance."

"You mean because of the rivalry between Sedgewood and Carnarvon?"

"No, it was more personal than that." Baines returned his gaze to Hale. "Back in '08, when Carter was a dealer in antiquities, he sold Lord Sedgewood a highly decorated bracelet from the tomb of Queen Ahhotep—the same tomb he later procured a dagger from. It turned out to be a fake, a copy of one in the Metropolitan Museum in New York."

Hale raised his eyebrows. "A fake! And what does Carter say about that?"

"Oh, he admits it, but he says it was an honest mistake. He refunded the money years ago. But His Lordship just won't let go of the incident. Apparently he showed the bracelet with some pride to an Egyptian lady of his acquaintance, who immediately identified it as a counterfeit. His Lordship was mortified. Every dealer and collector of antiquities in England knows the story. In fact, Mr. Hill was just asking me about it. His Lordship says it doesn't matter whether Carter is a crook or incompetent, he shouldn't have the rights to King Tut's tomb."

Hale thought it all over. "I can see where that would lead to a bit of unpleasantness between Carter and your patron, but what does it have to do with Alfie?"

"Whenever Mr. Barrington had a few drinks, he was not above bringing up the issue. To Carter it was like picking at a festering wound."

That fit. According to Carter's account, Alfie had questioned Carter's professionalism. Perhaps his verbal attack involved more than just the well-known fact that Carter was a self-made man.

"As it happens, Alfie was drinking on the evening of his murder," Hale said. "And he got into an argument with Carter at their club."

Baines sat back, looking satisfied with himself. "Well, there you have it, then! An enraged Howard Carter bided his time, but not very long, and stabbed Mr. Barrington later that night."

Hale could almost believe it. But what about the dagger missing from Lord Sedgewood's library, which Rollins apparently believed had been used to kill Alfie? Well, maybe Rollins was wrong about that. And maybe it had been missing for weeks and nobody noticed. If that were the case, it wouldn't be such a coincidence that the dagger was gone. But then there was that call to Scotland Yard about the weapon. How did that fit in? And who made the call, and why? Was Alfie in possession of the weapon and attacked someone who then disarmed him and turned the weapon about? Yes, that would explain the dagger being stolen, used, and unaccounted for. Could Alfie have attacked Carter and Carter merely defended himself?

Hale stood up. "You've certainly given me something to think about." *Entirely too much, in fact!*

"I'm glad to have been of service," Baines said, rising along with him. "I shouldn't wish any further unpleasantness to befall Lady Sarah."

The two men chatted meaninglessly as they walked toward the door. Hale paused for a moment to eye a small black bust, obviously Egyptian, sitting on a credenza in the hallway.

"Handsome woman," he observed.

"That's a small souvenir of my first dig with Lord Sedgewood. I was privileged to be at the discovery of the sepulcher of Thutmose III. It was very interesting. The sepulcher was found among the rocks near Habsepsus, the Great Goat Temple at Deir el-Bahari."

"When was that?"

"About twenty years ago. Let's see . . . March of '04, it would have been." He shook his head. "Hard to believe it's been that long."

"You must have been quite young, then. Where did you study archeology?"

Hale hadn't forgotten Howard Carter's accusation that Baines was as lacking in a university degree as Carter himself. He had just been waiting for an opportunity to ask about it without seeming to ask about it.

"Oxford," Baines said. "I was a student of the legendary Professor Courtland. Do you know him, by any chance?"

"I'm afraid not."

Not yet.

Later that afternoon, Hale returned to his office with the notes from the British Open that had been wired by Willie Gordon. The old pro had found so many quotable observers at the Open that, despite all that was weighing on his mind, Hale could hardly wait to start weaving them into a colorful feature story.

But he had hardly sat down at his typewriter when the telephone at his elbow rang.

"Hale."

"Oh, thank God, you're finally there." The high-pitched, frantic voice bordered on panic. "I've been calling every fifteen minutes."

"Sarah! What's wrong now?"

"It's Father. He's dead—murdered!"

FIFTEEN
Murder Calls Again

No one ever commits murder with a golden dagger.
— Hindu Proverb

They agreed to meet at the Museum Tavern on Great Russell Street, not far from Sarah's home. The venerable pub, expanded in the middle of the previous century, was actually older than the museum itself, having changed its name after the Museum was built in the 1760s. Karl Marx had been a patron, and Hale had once seen the writer Sir Arthur Conan Doyle having a pint at the bar.

Sarah was already there when Hale arrived. He gave her a discreet hug and a conventional, "I'm so sorry. What happened?" He sat down at her table.

"The parlor maid, Maisie, found his body crushed beneath one of the statues in the library—the one of the cat-headed Egyptian goddess Bastet. Maisie saw right away it couldn't have been an accident. It would have taken too much force to tip the statue over. She called the police and then she had the presence of mind to call me. I immediately telephoned Charles and then you."

Hale remembered the big statue well from his many uncomfortable encounters with Lord Sedgewood in that room. The Earl was a hard-driving man of property who didn't like journalists. Hale, for his part, had never been fond of the American aristocracy of which his family was a part, much less the British one. The only thing the two men agreed on was that they both loved Sarah. She was the only soft spot in her widower father's hard shell that Hale knew of.

"I want to go to the house as soon as possible," Sarah said. "I want you to go with me."

He shook his head. "We shouldn't be seen together, lest Rollins draw the wrong conclusion. In fact—"

"I wasn't followed here. I checked."

Hale allowed himself a half-smile. "Good girl. I wasn't either. Look, it's okay if you go to Carlton House Terrace. That would be perfectly normal. But Scotland Yard probably won't let you see the body." *It's got to be a bloody mess.*

"I want to go anyway, but I don't want to go alone."

"Then see if Charles will take you."

She licked her lips, as if thinking. "Yes, of course, Charles will take me. He's been such a rock for me through all this."

Still, Hale noted with satisfaction, she seemed disappointed that he wouldn't be the one at her side.

"I'll call Ned Malone and tell him what happened. He'll rush over to Carlton House Terrace to get the story. When he gets back to the office to write it up, I'll be there. He'll tell me everything."

"Such as what?"

Hale shrugged. "Whatever Rollins is willing to tell him. But we can't count on Scotland Yard, based on the Inspector's performance so far. It looks like we have to figure out who wanted to kill both Alfie and your father."

And immediately he had a candidate: Howard Carter. What was it that Baines had said? *"I've thought for a long time that Carter would kill His Lordship if he had the chance."*

But was it credible that Carter had killed Alfie in a rage and then decided to kill the father-in-law because of their long-simmering antagonistic relationship? And wouldn't the butler know if Carter had called on Sedgewood right before his murder? In fact, wouldn't he know if *anybody* had?

Hale suddenly realized that he didn't know how long Sarah had been trying to reach him.

"When did the maid find your father?"

"This afternoon, only about an hour and a half ago. She was the only other person in the house today. Daddy had given Reynolds the day off."

So the butler wasn't going to be any help after all.

"Rollins will say that's very convenient—the fact that Reynolds wasn't around and only family members were at the townhouse today."

Sarah's wide green eyes opened still wider. "He can't believe that one of us did it?"

"He already thinks that you and I killed Alfie, or at least that we're the most likely suspects. He doesn't strike me as the sort of man easily swayed from his conviction."

"But that's ridiculous. I loved Daddy. Why would I kill him?"

Hale noticed that she had slipped back into calling her father by the name that she had used for him when Hale had first met her—undoubtedly a vestige of a childhood that she was no longer so eager to escape.

He cleared his throat. "I don't think it would be hard for Inspector Rollins to find out that your father didn't want me for a son-in-law. And since Rollins thinks that you and I killed Alfie so that we could—"

Sarah jumped into his pause. "All right. I see what you mean." She swallowed. "It's not such a crazy notion, you know—that I would want to be with you."

Steady, Hale!

If he didn't block that happy line of thought out of his mind, he would never be able to concentrate on his next moves. He was thankful, therefore, for the Irish waitress who brought Sarah a cup of coffee and asked if he wanted something to drink. Seldom, if ever, had he felt in such need of a good slug of straight Old Forester. Kentucky bourbon being unavailable because of Prohibition, and the Irish and Scotch counterparts unpalatable, Hale ordered a Fuller's.

"There's something I have to tell you." Sarah looked down at the empty placemat in front of her, and then at Hale. "It's about the knife that killed Alfie."

This cannot be good.

"Father's dagger from the tomb of Ahhotep really *was* the murder weapon, just like the anonymous call to Inspector Rollins said."

"How do you know that?" Hale's tone was sharp and he didn't care.

"Please don't be angry with me, Enoch. I had to do it."

"Do what?"

Her eyes, already red and puffy from crying, held large pools of tears ready to spill over into her coffee cup.

She swallowed. "I—I hid the dagger." She looked down at the table and the tears that had been in her eyes splashed and made ripples in the coffee.

Hale felt himself redden. "What the—"

"I suppose it was wrong of me, but I didn't know what else to do." She was looking at him again and trying to dry her eyes with one of those silly lace handkerchiefs woman insist on carrying. Her hand trembled as she wiped her eyes. She breathed deeply before she continued.

"You know I stayed overnight at the townhouse on Monday after Charles and I had dinner with Daddy. But I couldn't sleep—who could, in my situation? I gave up about three in the morning and went into the library for something to read. As I was looking around, I noticed that the case with the Ahhotep dagger was slightly open. I went to close it and I saw that the dagger had dried blood on it. I almost fainted."

"Because you knew what that meant."

She nodded. "Of course I thought right away that Daddy must have used the dagger to stab Alfie. I had to protect Daddy. So I took the dagger away in my bag—just like Inspector Rollins thought, but not *when* he thought."

"Then what?"

"I buried it in my backyard. Nobody will ever find it there."

Hale leaned forward and lowered his voice. He wanted to shout. "That was a little detail you left out earlier, when you told me the dagger had been taken from the library. Not to put too fine a point on it, you lied to me, Lady Sarah."

The formal title was a deliberate slap, and Sarah seemed to feel it. She flinched.

"I didn't want to involve you."

"How could I be any more involved than I already am, you silly girl?"

"Here we are." The waitress set down Hale's ale. He forced a grateful smile and told the Irish girl they didn't want to order anything else just now.

"I deserved that," Sarah said when the waitress had left. "It *was* silly to do that. But, don't you see, I was still stunned from Alfie's death and lacking sleep. I wasn't thinking very clearly at all. I should have told you everything and let you take care of it."

Hale's anger drained out of him. "That would have been equally silly, I'm afraid. I haven't exactly covered myself with glory in this business. Maybe the answer was in front of me the whole time."

He thought back to Charles saying that even the governor wouldn't have killed Alfie for the company he kept, or something to that effect. Hale remembered thinking then that perhaps that was exactly what had happened—that Sedgewood could have killed his son-in-law during a heated argument. Maybe somebody else reached the same conclusion with more conviction, and killed Sedgewood in retribution. But who loved Alfie that much? Certainly not his wife—Hale felt that in his bones.

"When I could think more clearly," Sarah said, "I realized that Daddy never would have taken an Egyptian artifact out of the house. He certainly wouldn't have had it with him on the street outside the Constitutional Club. That means he didn't kill Alfie after all."

Hale wasn't so sure. "Maybe the two of them were in the library at the townhouse. Your father was examining the dagger at the time. They argued, and he thrust the weapon into Alfie before he even knew what he was doing. Then he moved the body later."

"I actually thought of that." Triumph shone in Sarah's green eyes. "So I talked to Reynolds. He was home that night—and so was Daddy. Daddy never went out. And Alfie wasn't at the townhouse that night."

Hale took a long pull on the dark brew, fervently wishing that it were something stronger. His head throbbed. "Let's recap: You found a bloody dagger in the library a little more than a day after somebody stabbed your husband to death. If His Lordship didn't use that dagger on Alfie, then who did?"

She was quiet for a moment. "I've thought a lot about that. I just don't know."

"It would have had to have been somebody who had access to your father's library both before and after the murder."

"You mean, like, one of the servants?"

No, that's not what I mean. Hale took another drink, for courage. He lit a panatela, stalling. "One of Alfie's friends"—it wouldn't help to mention the Woolfs—"suggested to me that maybe Charles was one of the many people who owed Alfie money."

Two years ago, when Hale had first met Charles without knowing who he really was, Dorothy Sayers had thought there was something fishy about him. Hale had never quite gotten over a negative prejudice against Sarah's brother, although Charles had always been nice enough to Hale. Was he the sort of man who could kill his brother-in-law to cancel out a big debt? Hale couldn't say no.

Sarah just looked at Hale, as though not believing what she had just heard.

"Well," Hale prodded. "Is it true? Did he owe Alfie?"

To his surprise, she smiled. "Who's being silly now? The situation is quite the reverse, I can assure you. Charles has had a very generous allowance from Daddy ever since their reconciliation. Alfie felt quite free to borrow money from him and lend it to his free-spending friends."

"Why does he have to borrow money? Isn't his father a duke?"

Her smile broadened. "Only a Yank would assume the two are contradictory." She sounded almost bemused. Hale wished he could see the humor. He could use a good laugh. "It turns out that the Duke of Somerset is a cash-poor aristocrat with nowhere near the money that Daddy imagined when he thrust Alfie at me. The family has property, but rents are low just now. Apparently the Somersets were not as industrious as the Sedgewoods. What I am saying is, Alfie and I are quite broke. Even Daddy never knew how broke, thanks to Charles helping us to keep up appearances."

An hour later, Ned Malone welcomed the news of Alfie Barrington's impecunious state as supporting his favorite theory.

"All the more reason that Alfie would have wanted to collect on money owed to him," he said. "And therefore, all the more likely that somebody unable to pay up settled the debt with a dagger to Alfie's heart."

They were sitting at Malone's desk at the Central Press Syndicate offices, where Hale had been waiting for him when he returned from the scene of the crime.

"Then why kill Lord Sedgewood?" Hale said. "And what about the fact that an Egyptian dagger of his probably was the murder weapon?" Hale had told Malone off the record, as a friend and not a journalist, everything he'd learned from Sarah. "How do you connect that?"

Malone shrugged. "There you have me. I don't have an answer for that. But Rollins does."

"I was afraid of that."

"His theory is that His Lordship knew that Lady Sarah killed Alfie, which made him dangerous to her. If Rollins knew that she'd buried the dagger—"

"I've been trying not to think about that. Say, does Rollins want you to publish that theory?"

Malone nodded.

"Good," Hale said. "That means he doesn't really have much."

"How do you figure that? I'd have thought just the opposite."

"No, he's trying to use you. He's hoping that if you publish that Sarah's the prime suspect, it will rattle her and cause her to make some big mistake—maybe move the hiding place of the missing dagger. I bet he puts her on round-the-clock watch."

Malone put a sheet of paper in his typewriter, ready to work on his story. "If that's the game Rollins is playing, I'm not the only one he's playing it with. Artie Howell from *The Times* got to the townhouse even before I did."

"Howell! How did he know about Sedgewood's murder?"

"Somebody tipped him off. I figure it must have been one of the servants."

Maisie had called Sarah right after she telephoned Scotland Yard. Reynolds, the butler, had worked for the family for decades. They seemed like loyal retainers.

"Why would they do that?" Hale wondered aloud.

But Malone was too busy pounding out his story on the Remington to answer.

SIXTEEN
The Curse Revisited

Curses come home to roost.
– King Alfred the Great, *Proverbs of Alfred*, 1275

Rathbone dropped around to Hale's desk on Saturday morning.

"Did you see this?" He held up the front section of *The Times*. Hale was sure he meant Artemis Howell's account of Lord Sedgewood's murder across the top of the front page, not the story on the side of the page about the American Walter Hagan's victory in the British Open the day before. (One old Scotsman, Hale knew, was going to be upset.)

"I read every word."

"More interesting than Malone's yarn, isn't it?"

"Maybe so," Hale acknowledged, "but Ned's isn't fiction." He nodded at the screaming headline: **THE CURSE OF AHHOTEP?**

The story, which Hale had consumed over breakfast at his flat before coming into the office, lived up to its breathless billing:

For the second time in less than a week, violent death has struck down a member of a noble family deeply involved in archeological excavations in the Valley of the Kings.

Edward Henry Bridgewater, 57, the fifth Earl of Sedgewood, was found Friday morning in the library of his Carlton House Terrace townhouse, crushed beneath a statue of the Egyptian goddess Bastet. The library housed much of his extensive collection of Egyptian artifacts.

Lord Sedgewood was the father-in-law of Alfred James Barrington, 29, who was stabbed to death Sunday evening near his club, the Constitutional. Sources say the Metropolitan Police, acting on information received, are investigating the possibility that he was stabbed with a dagger from the tomb of the ancient Egyptian Queen Ahhotep.

"We are pursuing several promising lines of inquiry," said Inspector Dennis Rollins. "Mummy's curses, witchcraft, and mumbo-jumbo are not among them."

But both dead men took part in a trip to Egypt in the summer of 1922 to negotiate a concession in the Valley of the Kings for the winter season. Sources close to the family say it was during that visit that Lord Sedgewood acquired by "less than legal means" the Queen Ahhotep dagger that may have been used to kill his son-in-law.

"I wonder who his sources 'close to the family' are?" Rathbone mused.

"This piece is mostly nonsense and the rest is pure speculation. And yet—" Hale frowned. "There does seem to be a definite Egyptian tinge to these doings. What worries me is that Sarah was on that voyage with Alfie and her father two years ago. She got married on the way back.

If these killings are somehow related to that, then Sarah might be in danger."

"Danger from whom? Or what? A stone statue with a cat's head?"

"I don't have any idea." Hale shook his head. "But not from a curse."

"Conan Doyle isn't so sure."

Howell's story had pulled out all the stops, from evoking the supposed "curse of the pharaohs" to interviewing Arthur Conan Doyle, one of Great Britain's most popular writers.

> Although skeptics may laugh, folklore says that anyone who opens the tomb of a pharaoh, whether grave-robber or archaeologist, will be repaid with illness, bad luck, or death. The best known example in modern times is the famous "King Tut's curse."
>
> Herbert George, Lord Carnarvon, died just four months after the opening of the tomb of the boy-king Tutankhamun. Four other men in some way associated with him have died in mysterious circumstances, including Lord Carnarvon's half-brother, the radiologist who x-rayed King Tut's mummy, and a visitor to the tomb.
>
> "I have long suspected that Lord Carnarvon's death was caused by elementals placed in Tutankhamun's tomb by his priests," opined the noted author and Spiritualist Sir Arthur Conan Doyle in an exclusive interview.
>
> Among hundreds of other works in a long and distinguished literary career, Conan Doyle is the author of "Lot 249," about the reanimation of an Egyptian mummy.

"As my fellow American, Henry Ford, might say: bunk!" Hale cried. "Conan Doyle's 'elementals,' whatever they are, are about as real as his mummy coming back from the dead. It all sounds like motion picture material to me."

"Bunk it may be, Hale, but it will sell newspapers for *The Times*." Rathbone's sharp features looked worried. "Our client newspapers are going to wonder why we aren't turning out copy like that."

"Well, don't look at me, Boss. You took me off the story, remember? If you want me back on it, just say—"

"There you are, Hale!"

Hale turned and saw, to his surprise, Howard Carter bearing down on him.

Carter stopped. "Oh, I see you're busy. I didn't mean to interrupt."

"Not at all," Hale said. "In fact, your timing is impeccable. I was just discussing King Tut's curse with my editor here, Mr. Nigel Rathbone."

Carter, turning purple, gave the South African a perfunctory handshake, and then burst out: "There is no curse! You saw that *Times* story? All stuff and nonsense! Lord Carnarvon was bitten on his cheek by a mosquito. He nicked the area while he was shaving and infection set in. That's what killed him—perfectly natural! But nobody listens to me. Look at me. I'm hale and hearty. If there was a curse, shouldn't I at least be wasting away?"

"What about the other four who died?" Rathbone said.

"Everybody has to die sometime! It was sheer coincidence of timing that their time came after the opening of the tomb. Aubrey Herbert, Lord Carnarvon's half-brother, died of blood poisoning after having his teeth extracted because some idiot told him it would restore his eyesight. That was a tragedy, but hardly a curse. Colonel Herbert didn't even have anything to do with Tutankhamun."

Hale couldn't resist the impulse to play devil's advocate. "If there were a curse, it would work through natural means, wouldn't it?"

"There is no curse." Carter wiped his forehead with a handkerchief. "I came here to presume on our acquaintance, Hale. I was hoping to get your assurance that the Central Press Syndicate won't follow *The Times* down this rabbit hole of curse rubbish. I'd like to see the contagion contained to one paper."

Not much chance of that, Hale thought. "Why do you care so much?"

Carter seemed to hesitate. Hale suspected that he was trying to figure out how frank to be. "Every time that sort of talk gets revived it makes it harder for me to find sponsors for new expeditions. What wealthy patron wants to be the latest victim of a so-called curse? Having a lot of money and a good family doesn't necessarily translate to having a lot of sense."

"I can't say I believe in King Tut's curse myself," Rathbone said, "but it's not journalism's business to sort out spiritual claims. There's still a significant reader interest in the boy-king. I can't promise that the CPS won't find a story in Lord Sedgewood's well-known rivalry with the late Lord Carnarvon." He fingered his bent pipe. "Of course, we would like to approach it from a different angle than the *Times* story, give our subscribers something fresh."

Carter's mustache twitched. "Like what?"

"Oh, I don't know—"

"I heard there was bad blood between you and Sedgewood long before his rivalry with Carnarvon or Alfie Barrington's efforts to get control of Tut's tomb for Baines," Hale said. "I was told it involved something you sold Sedgewood years ago."

To Hale's surprise, the archeologist seemed unconcerned. "Yes, that's true. It happened well over fifteen years ago, when I was still quite young. I was taken in by a counterfeit of a bracelet belonging to Ahhotep. Sedgewood was always fascinated by that particular queen, for some reason, so I offered it to him and he bought it. When he found out that it wasn't genuine, I apologized, returned his money, and wrote an article about my mistake so that others might profit by it. I imagine that just about everyone in the field knows the story as a sort of footnote to my otherwise successful career, but the only one it matters to is—*was*—Sedgewood. He could always be relied on to bring it up in some snide way when we chanced across each other. I was beyond even being annoyed by it at this point."

Rathbone gave Hale a look that said: *No story there. And no motive for murder, either.* If the episode was as widely known as Carter professed, then he certainly wouldn't have killed Sedgewood to shut him up.

"I say, Hale, did you talk to Baines as I suggested?" Carter asked.

"I've been too busy with work," Hale lied. "Mr. Rathbone runs a tight ship."

And at the same time he thought: Talking to Baines wasn't enough. He was too eager to point the finger at Carter. His credentials deserve further investigation.

SEVENTEEN
Looking for Answers

A scholar knows nothing of boredom.
— Jean Paul Richter, *Hesperus*, 1795

Hale went downstairs to the Syndicate's morgue, which contained files of clippings from every major British and European newspaper.

"I need anything you can find on an Oxford don named Courtland," he told the librarian, a great bear of a man with bushy eyebrows named Trosley.

Trosley smiled through his salt and pepper beard. "Victim of a crime or the perpetrator?"

"Neither, so far as I know. But I don't know much yet."

Trosley brought back a file so thick it took Hale an hour to read it. Although Hale had never heard of the man, the Press had spilled quite a bit of ink on him over the years. He spoke seven languages, including Turkish, Arabic, and Greek, and had used them for more than writing in academic journals. There were as many stories of him riding camels with T.E. Lawrence in Arabia and finding lost cities in Jordan as there were of him delivering lectures at international conferences. He must be in his seventies by now, but showed few signs of slowing down. He'd just returned to England from a year at Harvard University as a visiting professor in Egyptology.

Hale walked into Rathbone's office with Courtland's file in his hand. "I have an idea for a new angle on the Egyptian business."

Rathbone put down his pen and picked up his pipe. "Good. Tell me."

Hale sat. "There's a fellow at Oxford named Walter Courtland who's the final word on all things Egyptian. He's not only stuck his nose in musty old books translating demotic and hieroglyphics, but also been in some tight places doing field work. Apparently Linwood Baines, Lord Sedgewood's counterpart to Carter, studied under him. I bet he's seen some strange things. He probably won't buy into the idea of a curse, unless he's gone round the bend like Conan Doyle. But if his past interviews are any indication, he'll have something quotable to say."

Rathbone offered a rare smile. "You'll do anything to get a piece of this story, won't you, Hale? Well, I admire your initiative. Enjoy Oxford!"

The train from Paddington Station to Oxford took sixty-one minutes, passing from city blight to suburban sprawl to the relatively open areas of Oxford.

Hale was surrounded by stately old buildings every day in London, but somehow it was only in towns like Winchester and Oxford that he felt the weight of history. Oxford had had a University Chancellor seven hundred years ago. The first universities in the American colonies, by contrast, hadn't set up shop until the seventeenth century. His own alma mater, Yale, was even later at 1701.

As Hale walked from the train station, he could well imagine his friend Dorothy Sayers making her way by foot or bicycle through these venerable streets in her college years. She'd been one of the first women to officially graduate from Oxford University. His favorite poem of hers was one that she'd written about her last morning as a student. How did it end?

> The thing that I remember most of all
> Is the white hemlock by the garden wall.

Hale found Professor Walter Courtland ensconced in his office in a fifteenth-century building on High Street. It was part of Magdalen College. Oscar Wilde had been an undergraduate at Magdalen, and Bertie Wooster more recently.

Courtland was bent over an ancient oak desk, writing in a notebook, when Hale stuck his head in. "Professor Courtland?"

He peered at Hale over half-moon glasses, a barrel-chested man whose tie was too short to travel the length of his stomach. Despite his short gray hair, he looked a decade younger than his age.

"That's what they call me. You must be Enoch Hale. Have a seat right there." He pointed at a chair that was already occupied. "Just stack the books on the floor."

His affable manner immediately shot down Hale's expectation that the Egyptologist would be an old curmudgeon like Ned Malone's friend Professor Challenger.

"You were a bit vague on the phone, Hale. On purpose, I expect. What do you want to talk to me about? I'm guessing mummies, mumbo-jumbo, something like that. Am I right?"

Hale smiled. "Something like that. How did you guess?"

Courtland snorted. "I didn't guess. I expected the Press to come calling as soon as I saw that pharaoh's curse story in this morning's *Times*. The many Press interviews that I have endured over the years have done my career no harm at all, I must admit." *That's why Trosley's file on you is so thick*, Hale thought. "So, ask away, young man. What do you want to know?"

Hale pulled out his Moleskine notebook. "Well, let's get basic. As an Egyptologist, what do you think of the curse of King Tut?"

"Nonsense."

Hale appreciated Courtland's concise clarity, but he needed more than a one-word answer. "You mean because Lord Carnarvon died of an infection?"

Courtland shook his head. "No, no, that's not what I mean. Of course, as an Egyptologist who has also done field work in archeology, I consider myself a scientist. Therefore, I see no reason not to believe the medical experts who determined infection to be the physical cause of Carnarvon's death. But that says nothing about any possible spiritual cause."

Hale scribbled like mad. "Please go on, Professor."

"I'll give you an example. Suppose I was deathly ill and I asked you to pray for my recovery. And suppose I recovered. My doctor would say that happy outcome was the result of his expert treatment and perhaps the administration of a new drug. You would say it was because of prayer." He shrugged. "Who really knows? But I would venture to say that you're both right. Aren't prayers usually answered by natural means? Science and religion are just two different ways of understanding the world, and not always mutually contradictory."

"You're a religious man, then?"

Courtland grinned. "So were Roger Bacon and Gregor Mendel. They were both friars, you know, and also rather good scientists. Some of the greatest scientists of the last century drew big headlines by embracing the Spiritualist faith, including Sir William Crookes, Alfred Russell Wallace, and Oliver Lodge."

Hale had known that. "But didn't that just prove they'd gone dotty near the end of their lives?"

"By no means, my boy! Crookes was at the height of his powers when he became a Spiritualist. He was initiated into the Hermetic Order of the Golden Dawn, an occult society, years before he was knighted for his considerable scientific achievements. I don't myself believe in Spiritualism, you understand. I find it hard enough in this country to be a Roman Catholic."

Hale decided it was time to back up. "So when you called the curse idea 'nonsense,' you were giving a personal opinion and not speaking as a scientist?"

Courtland glanced around at the books that lined three of the four walls of his office, as if in thought. "I spoke as an Egyptologist highly familiar with the tomb of Tutankhamun. I can assure that the Carnarvon expedition didn't activate a curse upon anyone who opened the tomb because *there was no such curse inscribed on the tomb.* Pharaohs depended on secret locations and hidden rooms to protect their bodies, not curses. The notion of the pharaoh's curse seems to be largely a nineteenth-century phenomenon."

Hale, stunned, couldn't write fast enough. Professor Courtland served up one great quote after another, bless him.

"Are you saying that no pharaoh ever put a curse on anyone who disturbed his tomb?"

Courtland smiled. "Well, certainly Tutankhamun didn't. In the few instances where there are curses on tombs, they appear to be directed at the *ka* priests as a warning to do their job properly."

"Then where did this idea of the curse of King Tut come from?"

"Journalism is your business, not mine, Mr. Hale, but I suspect that headlines containing the word 'curse' sold quite a few newspapers after Carnarvon died."

Hale remembered all the stories about Tut that Reggie Lestrange of his own syndicate had cranked out. But even Reggie had to have something to work with. "Reporters didn't make up all those deaths that followed the opening of Tut's tomb."

"No, but they *connected* them, they provided a link and a narrative that turned several isolated tragedies into a curse. I'll give you another example to illustrate what I mean. Suppose that the Duke of Marlborough died tomorrow. You might barely note the fact, unless he was a friend of yours. Now, suppose that in the middle of next week the motion picture actor Rudolph Valentino died. You might be shocked because he is so young. But you wouldn't connect his death to the Duke's demise—*unless someone told you that famous persons died in threes*. In that case, I assure you, you would find a third death before long."

Courtland's point scored with Hale in a way that the professor could never know. In Hale's two years with Sarah, she had often insisted that the death of notable personages came in threes. They had on more than one occasion quarreled playfully as to whether a certain deceased was sufficiently famous to qualify as the third in a series.

Hale asked a few more questions, then closed his notebook and stood up. Sometimes the most important questions in interviews came after he did that, when the subject was relaxed and off-guard.

"Curse or not," he said, "you must have had a strong interest in the activities of Lord Sedgewood. I understand that his man Linwood Baines was a student of yours."

Courtland shook his head. "Not so."

"No?"

"No."

"Maybe you just don't remember him."

The professor assumed a self-satisfied look that Hale hadn't seen him display until now. "I remember all my students, Mr. Hale. I have a bit of a reputation for that. Still, when I heard that Baines was saying that he studied under me, I worried that perhaps my memory is slipping. And in forty-one years at Oxford, I've had a lot of students. So I looked up the records just to be certain. I can assure you that Linwood Baines never attended Magdalen College—or, I venture to say, any other college."

Hale almost smiled. *Now I'm getting somewhere*, he thought. He'd caught Baines in a provable lie, no ambiguity. But almost immediately he wondered about something.

"How did you know that Baines is telling people you were his teacher?"

"That's an odd thing, Mr. Hale. I just had a visit a couple of days ago from another gentleman asking me about Mr. Baines."

Hale's eyebrows shot up. "You mean another reporter? Or was it a Scotland Yard detective?"

"Neither. It was a man named Mr. Burton Hill. He professed to be a collector of Egyptian antiquities, which—based on his obvious ignorance of the subject—he most certainly is not."

EIGHTEEN
Re-Partnering

What is food to one man may be poison to another.
– Lucretius, *De rerum natura*, 57 B.C.

Burton Hill! In his mind's eye Hale could see the bulky, elderly gentleman who had been leaving Baines's house just as he'd arrived. Apparently he'd also been checking out the archaeologist's story—but why?

Hale spent half the trip back to London trying to figure that out before giving it up as a bad job. He finally decided that he needed to learn *who* before he could have a chance at knowing *why*. Who was Burton Hill? That question he could pursue at the office. Meanwhile, he spent the second half of the train trip organizing his feature story on Professor Walter Courtland, man of science and faith but not superstition.

Trosley was on his way out the door when Hale arrived at Fleet Street. Hale tried to talk the librarian into staying a few extra minutes to help him do some research.

"Sorry, Hale." He didn't look sorry. "I promised my wife I wouldn't be home late again tonight. It is Saturday, after all. You know where the morgue key is. Turn out the light when you've finished."

An hour later, Hale was unsurprised to learn that not a single clipping about Mr. Burton Hill appeared in the thousands of files of the Central Press Syndicate morgue. After all, the great majority of solid citizens go through their entire lives without having their names published in a newspaper. What was that old line? "A lady only has her name in the newspaper three times—when she's born, when she marries, and when she dies." It was far less likely, however, that Mr. Hill's name wouldn't appear in any of the dozens of telephone books leaning against the east wall of the library. But it didn't. Among the Hills there had been one Bart, a Beatrice, two Benjamins, two Brendans, and four Bruces, but no Burton.

Hale strongly suspected that Burton Hill was about as real as Prudence Beresford. And Hale was no closer than when he'd begun at learning what the old fellow was up to.

After dinner, Hale brooded in the small sitting room of his flat. He couldn't shake the fear that whoever had it in for Sarah's husband and her father might have Sarah in his sights as well. His reverie was jarred by the ringing of his telephone. Calls in the evening were seldom good news.

"Hale? This is Charles. Sarah is terribly ill. The doctor is with her now, but she wants to see you. Can you come over to Carlton House Terrace right away?"

Hale hesitated for a moment. It didn't seem a good idea to be running to Sarah at her late father's townhouse while the two of them were under suspicion, and perhaps under surveillance. But, damn it, Sarah was calling for him.

"Of course. I'll be right there."

He was halfway out the door before he realized he hadn't asked exactly what was wrong with Sarah.

Charles Bridgewater, the newly minted Lord Sedgewood, met him at the door. Portia Lyme, Charles's red-haired fiancée, stood behind him. Reynolds, the family butler, was nowhere in sight.

"How is she, your Lordship?" The sixth Earl of Sedgewood seemed somewhat startled at the question. Perhaps that was the first time anyone had called Charles by his just-inherited title.

"We're waiting for the doctor to tell us."

"What's wrong with her?"

"We don't know, exactly, just that she became quite sick very suddenly. It started a few hours ago with a stomach ache, cold sweats, weak muscles, and dizziness. She staggered when she walked. When she vomited, I insisted on calling Dr. Johnson."

A tall man with an impressive head of cotton-white hair and a doctor's bag in his hand came out of the parlor, closing the pocket doors behind him. He said to Charles: "That was too close for my comfort. Good thing I was at home when you called me."

"Was she really that bad off?"

"She could have died. A few minutes would have made all the difference."

Sarah's brother looked stricken. "What was it?"

"Some sort of food poisoning, I suppose."

"But we all ate the same thing," Portia said. She didn't look like she ever ate much at all, Hale thought. She weighed all of—what?—ninety-eight pounds, maybe.

The doctor looked skeptical. "Odd. Well, at any rate, I gave her an emetic, a purgative, and brandy. Your parlor maid was kept quite busy emptying chamber pots. Lady Sarah won't be dancing the Charleston anytime soon. You can go in and see her, but try not to get her upset."

"Thank you, Dr. Johnson. I'll see you out."

Does the butler have another night off? Hale wondered. *And why am I even worried about that when Sarah could have died?*

"It's just like what happened to Carnarvon," Portia stage-whispered. "Mysterious illness. *I* think it's a curse, like it said in *The Times*. Isn't that just divine?"

Divine! Hale thought. "There's nothing mysterious about a mosquito bite," he said in lieu of slapping her. "Or food poisoning." But how could it be food poisoning if . . .

Charles returned. "Are you ready to see her, Hale? This won't be pretty."

"I'm ready."

Sarah lay on the settee, where—Hale later learned—she had collapsed. Parlor pillows were placed behind her and her white evening frock was wrinkled and disheveled. The organdy material fell to about eight inches above her ankles and a light green sash of crisp taffeta circled her waist. It was the perfect color to match her eyes. Sarah's shoes sat at the end of the settee and her feet were tucked up near her body. Her face was the color of the keys on the piano in the parlor. She favored Hale with a weak smile. "I knew you'd come."

"How do you feel?"

"Ghastly, but better now that you're here."

Portia Lyme put her arm through her fiancé's. "Come on, Charles. I think these two want to be alone."

Sarah smiled weakly. "Thank you, Charles. You were right."

"I'd have rather been wrong." He bent over and kissed his sister on the forehead. "I feel so bad about this." He turned to Hale. "You mustn't stay long, you know. She needs her rest."

"I promise."

Sarah waited until Charles and Portia had gone before she spoke. "Dear Charles! The doctor said he saved my life. I couldn't believe there was anything that wrong with me. Charles himself was slightly ill this morning. I thought I just had a touch of the same thing."

"Why did you summon me here?"

"Because, my darling, when Dr. Johnson told me it was very, very serious, I was afraid that I might die without ever seeing you again. Right now, you are my only friend and protection. I need you with me."

Hale moved toward her, but stopped. *Not now, Enoch.* "I think you would do well to remember that your husband was murdered less than a week ago." He tried to sound stern, even though he felt weak.

She shuddered and looked both hurt and confused. "I'm not likely to forget, am I? Those men from Scotland Yard keep coming back and asking me questions over and over again."

"Well, I've been asking questions of my own and I think I'm on to something." He pulled over a chair and sat down in front of Sarah, trying not to look at her shapely ankles. "Linwood Baines tells people that he studied under the highly-respected Walter Courtland at Oxford, but he didn't. He didn't study at Oxford at all!"

Hale's bombshell didn't get the reaction he expected.

Sarah chuckled.

"Daddy knew that, of course. Everybody knew that. It was just Baines's way of trying to get one up on Howard Carter. It was practically a joke, and poor Baines was the only one not in on it. Nobody cares that he doesn't have a university degree—except him. So we all pretend that we believe his nonsense about his days at Oxford."

Hale put his head in his hands. "So Baines had no reason to kill Alfie or your father to hide his secret, because it wasn't a secret?" He looked at the hat he still held in his hands while he thought for a moment. "But wait, if Baines was the only one who wasn't in on the joke, then he must have thought people believed his tale. And if he believed his secret was about to be given away by Alfie or your father, he might kill either or both of them."

"I hadn't thought of it like that," Sarah said. "But surely, he had every reason to wish Daddy good health. With Daddy dead, Baines will have to find himself a new patron."

With an effort, Hale concentrated on the remaining options. "Either your father knew who killed Alfie and had to be eliminated for the killer's protection, or he killed Alfie and somebody killed him in revenge."

"Daddy had nothing to do with Alfie's murder. I told you that." Despite the weakness in her voice, she spoke sharply.

"Did your father give you any hint that he might have known who killed Alfie?"

Sarah shook her head. "Not at all. He seemed as baffled as I was."

Hale tossed his hat on the settee next to Sarah. "Okay, well maybe somebody *thought* your father killed Alfie."

Sarah lifted herself up on one elbow. "Like who, Enoch? Who would want to avenge Poor Alfie? His parents and his older brother are dead, his sister lives in New York, and I don't believe those Bloomsbury people really gave a fig for him."

"What's that mark on your right hand?" Sarah had such beautiful hands.

She looked at it. "It's nothing. A bug bite, I suppose."

Like Lord Carnarvon. Hale exiled the thought from his mind as soon as it made its unwanted appearance. For that way lay madness. Frustrated, he punched his fist into his other hand. "Damn it, Sarah! You didn't kill Alfie and your father, and I sure as hell didn't do it. But unless I figure out who did, Rollins is going to try to pin it on us."

"I'll help you, Enoch! We can do this together." *Just like Tommy and Tuppence.* "I could even wear a disguise. I know all about make-up from my music hall days, you know."

He smiled, charmed by her naivety despite his foul mood. "I don't think that will be necessary. Just help me think this through. We need to pick up on loose ends, things that don't fit or don't make sense." He thought a second. "Have you ever heard of a man named Burton Hill?"

"No. Who is he?"

"That's what I'd like to know. He was coming out of Baines's house just as I got there, and then when I interviewed Professor Courtland I found out that he'd been there before me asking questions. He claims to be a collector of Egyptian antiquities, but Courtland said he didn't know the first thing about the subject."

"Perhaps he's some sort of private investigator."

That made sense, of a sort, but who would hire such a person? Or would the killer himself investigate his own killing and leave a false trail for others to follow? *Only in an Agatha Christie or Dorothy Sayers detective novel!*

Hale mentally turned the page on that subject.

"Maybe we need to get back to basics. Let's think about the night that Alfie died. You told me that Reynolds said your father didn't go out that night and Alfie didn't come here. Reynolds also had the day off on Friday, when your father was killed. If I were a cynical fellow, I might say that was very convenient. I'd like to talk to him. Where is he today? Your brother opened the door himself."

"Reynolds quit without notice."

"What! When?"

"Just this morning. He said he'd been offered another position a few days ago, and with Daddy's death he decided that he should take it."

Hale stood up. "Now I'd really like to see Reynolds. What is this new position?"

"He didn't say."

NINETEEN
On the Links

"Two people rarely see the same thing."
– Agatha Christie, *Murder on the Links*, 1923

With Sarah's strength visibly fading, Hale left soon after.

His fitful sleep was shattered the next morning by the ringing of his telephone. If this kept up, he would have the damned thing pulled out.

"Yeah?" he said groggily.

"Good morning, Enoch. It's Prudence Beresford."

That woke him up. He didn't appreciate being reminded of how she'd made a fool of him.

"Forgive me if I don't see the humor, Mrs. Christie."

"I'm sorry. Force of habit. This isn't exactly a social call. Your plight has been much on my mind as I've felt wretched about leaving you in the lurch. When I read about this new tragedy, Lord Sedgewood's murder, I knew I had to take some action. So I've been making some inquiries."

Good grief! Another amateur sleuth enters the mix! Hale summoned his patience. "I'm sure you're trying to help, and I appreciate your good intentions—"

"There's someone I think you need to talk to."

"Who?"

"Your flat is on Claverton Street, near St. George Square, right?"

"Yes, but—"

"I'll pick you up in my Morris Cowley at one o'clock. And wear your golfing clothes!"

She hung up.

Golfing clothes? Damn the woman!

Hale's attitude had not improved any when Agatha Christie pulled up in her gray bullnose Morris Cowley automobile with the top down at the appointed hour. She surely looked the part of the modern sportswoman, with a horizontal striped teal and yellow belted sweater over a white blouse and a pleated white skirt with large buttons that ran down the side. For headgear she wore a white straw snap-brimmed hat that had a ribbon of matching material from the sweater. *Quite stunning, really.* Pushing the thought away, Hale got in and slammed the door. A set of golf clubs occupied the tonneau.

"Where the hell are we going?"

"Sunningdale."

Hale stared as she confidently stepped on the gasoline pedal. "You actually want to play golf?"

"That's just our cover to get us to the nineteenth hole."

The fish-out-of-water confusion that Hale felt made him even more testy. "What about your husband? You do remember that you have a husband, Mrs. Christie?"

Her face clouded. "He's off on one of his golfing weekends. Or so he says. Well, we shall play some golf of our own. How is Mrs. Barrington holding up?"

"Not very damned well, but thanks for asking." He quickly described Sarah's symptoms and the weak condition in which he'd left her the night before.

Agatha shot him a glance. "That sounds like nicotine poisoning."

"Nicotine is poison? Really poison? I didn't know that."

"Oh, yes. It can be quite deadly in the right amount—and easy to obtain. Something like arsenic or strychnine may be traceable. Someone who buys rat poison or gets arsenic at the chemist for killing bees has to sign for it. But one can procure enough nicotine to kill from a single pack of cigarettes."

That sounded too simplistic to Hale. "Doesn't that take some special knowledge or equipment?"

Agatha shook her head, her hair flying from the wind that surrounded the open car. "Not at all. One just removes the paper and places the tobacco from the cigarettes in a small pot of boiling water. Pour the boiling mixture in a jar, put the cover on and let it sit overnight. In the morning decant the liquid through some cheesecloth, squeeze the liquid all out, and discard the residue. Now slowly boil the liquid down to a kind of semi-solid jelly. You have almost pure nicotine and no one knows it."

"But how do you get someone to take it. Isn't it bitter, like tobacco?"

"Somewhat," she replied as she downshifted and roared past a Bentley. "But one doesn't have to eat it to be poisoned. One could do that, of course, but one can also get quite ill just handling it—the skin absorbs it—or by inhaling the fumes when it's boiling down."

Hale was suddenly very glad that he hadn't got too close to this woman with such a grisly turn of mind. "How do you know this stuff?"

She smiled. "Murder is my business. And I've been intrigued by nicotine poisoning since the War. In the dispensary, I once saw a soldier mad with shell-shock get sick from eating tobacco."

"Well, we're a long way from 1918. You should use nicotine in one of your books, but I'm not convinced that someone used it on Sarah."

"What else, then—coincidence or curse?"

Hale had no answer for that. And if Agatha was right, it meant that whoever killed Sarah's husband and father also wanted to do away with her.

In about fifty minutes they arrived at Sunningdale.

"I do hope we can get on the new course designed by Harry Colt," Agatha remarked as she swung into the club's parking area.

"Oh, there he is!" she exclaimed.

A medium-size man with short hair and aquiline features, wearing a black suit, stood near the putting green. As they drew closer, Hale realized that he wore a clerical collar.

"Is that the person you want me to meet? Or should I say the parson?"

"No, we're just playing golf with him. I brought you a set of clubs, by the way."

After parking the car, Agatha led Hale over to the man. "This is Father Ronald Knox, chaplain at St Edmund's College in East Hertfordshire, the oldest Roman Catholic school in England." That seemed to Hale an odd sort of friend for Agatha Christie to have. Had she gone to him for marriage counseling? As if reading his mind Agatha added, "He's quite the detective story buff."

That was proved by the discussion that accompanied their movement from hole to hole.

Knox had already procured caddies and, after shaking hands with Hale, insisted that they must hurry. "We had best not be late. We only have a few minutes to start. They are very strict around here about tee times."

Hale was not looking forward to playing. He had only played three or four times since coming to England. Before that had been the war—not much golfing there.

Knox stepped up and addressed the ball on the first tee. "This course starts with a par four, Mr. Hale. It is 465 yards to the hole. I would recommend you try to keep your ball to the right on the fairway." So saying, Knox drove his ball about 180 yards to the exact place he had pointed out to Hale.

"I hope that I can give the two of you some competition, Father," Hale remarked as he set his ball to tee off. "I don't play much and when I did my handicap ran eighteen."

"I'm sure you will do fine, Mr. Hale. What's your handicap these days, Agatha?"

Agatha laughed out loud. "You know very well it is a miserable thirty-five. Now go ahead, Mr. Hale, and start so we can move up to the women's tee box."

Hale hit to the right just as Knox had recommended—so far right he was somewhere in the trees. "Nice slice," Hale muttered to himself.

As they walked down the fairway after Agatha put her shot just short and to the left of Knox's ball, she started to direct the conversation.

"The detective story is a game, just like golf," Agatha said, "so it must have rules."

"Perhaps it would not even be blasphemous to call them commandments," Father Knox suggested.

"But rules can be broken."

"So can commandments, but with more severe consequences."

"What are these rules of the detective story?" Hale asked, just to keep his hand in as he started to look for his ball. He had resigned himself to a waiting game. Whatever Agatha had in mind would unfold in due time.

"That's the devil of it," Father Knox said. "No one knows what the rules are. They haven't been written yet, but they will be[4]. They must. Detective stories are more popular than mahjong right now, but anybody can write anything—secret passages, detectives who turn out to be murderers. Someone has to bring order to it!"

"I'd like to see you try," Agatha said. "Everyone may agree that there should be rules, but no one will agree on what those rules should be. For example, I have this notion of making the narrator of my Hercule Poirot stories the killer. No one would suspect him! But I'm certain that some readers would say that's against the rules which haven't been written."

Father Knox laid his second shot just off the green to the left.

"You can't do that, Agatha! It's just not cricket! The first commandment of detective fiction should be that the killer mustn't be anyone whose thoughts we are allowed to share."

"Why not?"

"Because the killer would be naturally thinking about his crime, so if we're going to peer into his thoughts that's what should be there."

"He wouldn't be thinking about it all the time, especially before the murder. And in my idea, the narrator is deliberately concealing some of his thoughts as a kind of game to fool the reader until the end of the book. Everything that he says is true; he just doesn't tell the reader everything."

Father Knox remained unconvinced. And on it went. Hale tuned out. At some point he realized that the topic had switched to the use of Orientals and twins in detective stories. Father Knox was against both.

---

[4] And they were – by Monsignor Knox himself, with tongue in check. See p. 176.

"But if they exist in real life, why not in fiction?" Hale objected.

The clergyman gave him a pitying look. "My dear fellow, the truth is no excuse. Fiction must be believable, even if it's based on something that really happened. No fiction writer would dare serve up some of the stories I've heard in the confessional. So I say sinister Orientals and convenient twins are out on the grounds of implausibility."

"How do you feel about servants?" Agatha asked.

"I don't have any, save the housekeeper, and she isn't a very good one. Bless her soul, she does try, though." Swinging too hard, he chipped over the green. "Have to come back now, won't I?"

"No, no. I mean servants as killers or witnesses."

"You mean, 'the butler did it'?"

"Actually," Agatha said reflectively, "that would be a bit of a surprise, wouldn't it? I mean, has any butler in fiction ever actually done it?"

Father Knox appeared to think about it. "I don't recall any, come to think of it."

"In real life, there was that Musgrave Ritual business that Sherlock Holmes solved as a young man," Hale said. He had immersed himself in Dr. Watson's accounts of the great detective soon after meeting him. "The Musgrave butler was the villain—but that wasn't murder."

"And besides, as Father Knox said, real life doesn't count," Agatha pointed out with a note of triumph in her voice. "At any rate, I did have a point. People don't pay attention to servants, either in fiction or in life. They should, you know. When I was young we had a lot of servants, and I learned ever so much from them. Who knows more about what's happening in a house than the servants? They see everything, and don't think they don't talk about it with each other even if it goes no further. The gossip upstairs among the family is nothing to what's going on downstairs among the servants. That's why I paid a call at the tradesman's entrance to Number 10 Carlton House Terrace this morning."

Surely Hale was dreaming this. "You did *what?*"

"You heard me. Lord Sedgewood was killed in his own home. Who would know more about it than his servants? I talked to the cook and the maid. It turned out that Brigid, the maid, adored my second novel, *The Secret Adversary*—quite the romantic, that one! How disappointing that she knew so little. And do you know who I didn't talk to?"

"Harley Reynolds, the butler," Hale snapped. "He quit."

"Quite so. But I found out where he went."

"You did?"

"Yes, but that will wait. It's a beautiful day and there are seventeen more holes to play. Lay on MacKnox! You've only won one hole so far."

Hale was frustrated, which didn't help his game any. By the time they finished the eighteenth hole, he was down nineteen shillings to the good father. Leaving their bags with the caddies, Father Knox recommended a trip to the clubhouse bar.

Of all the surprises in that day of surprises, the biggest was the sight of the man mixing drinks behind the bar. At about six-foot-five, he looked more like a prizefighter than a bartender—or the butler that he had formerly been.

"Reynolds!" Hale exclaimed.

Lord Sedgewood's ex-servant smiled in recognition. "Mr. Hale—good to see you, sir!" The two had met on many occasions, the first being when Sarah's father had had the butler throw Hale out of his townhouse after their first encounter almost four years earlier. Hale could scarcely believe that the man he had most wanted to talk with was standing behind the bar on a golf course.

"Whatever are you doing here?" he asked.

Reynolds straightened up. "I'm the assistant steward, sir."

"Congratulations. Lady Sarah told me that you'd left the family's service, but she didn't know why."

Reynolds looked around, leaned forward, and spoke in a low voice. "It was the curse, sir. I got the heebie-jeebies being in that house after the old Earl was killed. Suppose that old mummy had bad aim and zapped me next by mistake!"

"Curse be damned!" Father Knox exploded. "Superstitious drivel! That should be another commandment for detective stories—no ghosts."

"A Roman priest is a fine one to be talking about superstition," Reynolds sniffed. "Even Mr. Charles—Lord Sedgewood, as he is now—said there might be something to the curse. I heard him talking on the telephone about it after His Lordship's body was found."

Hale found it hard to believe that Reynolds had that right. Charles must have been displaying an unsuspected penchant for black humor in a call to a friend. At any rate, Hale had more important questions to ask.

"Listen, Reynolds," he said, "someone tipped Scotland Yard that Sedgewood's dagger might have been the murder weapon. And somebody—likely the same person—told that sap Howell at *The Times* that the dagger was contraband. Was it you?"

The assistant steward looked offended. "Certainly not! No one in service would have done such a thing. Besides, how would I know anything about it?"

"Well, you might have been the one who used the dagger on Alfie Barrington."

Reynolds's jaw dropped. If the man was not utterly shocked at the suggestion, he was the greatest actor since William Gillette.

"Me, sir? But that's ridiculous. Why would I have done a thing like that?"

Hale sighed. He could think of no reason in the world why the butler would have done it. None of the usual motives fit—blackmail, romantic jealousy, money. Unless—

"Pounds sterling might have something to do with it," Hale said. "Suppose Alfie's death was a smoke screen and Lord Sedgewood was the real victim all along. Did he leave you a legacy?"

"I—I have no idea, sir." Sweat poured out Reynolds's craggy forehead.

"I like that idea," Agatha said. "May I use it?"

Ignoring her, Hale continued to address Reynolds. "It's quite convenient that you had the day off when Sedgewood was killed, thereby making it look that you weren't around at the time."

"His Lordship let me off to visit my brother in Lancashire. He's quite ill."

"Maybe," Hale said skeptically. "That can be checked. If that's true, who would know you were away that day?"

"The rest of the staff, of course. His Lordship may have mentioned it to his family. And perhaps Lady Lawrence."

"Who?"

"Lady Lydia Lawrence—His Lordship's, er, friend. She and His Lordship often met alone at the townhouse, or sometimes at the country estate, but quite discreetly. Even Lady Sarah and Mr. Charles don't know." He leaned forward and whispered. "She is a married woman, you see."

TWENTY
Chamber of Horrors

One day men will look back and say I gave birth to the
Twentieth Century.
— Jack the Ripper, *Letter to Police*, 1888

That evening, Hale walked down Fleet Street
toward the Cheshire Cheese pub with Agatha's
recriminations still ringing in his ears.

"You should be ashamed of yourself!" she'd
thundered as they climbed back into her car. "You scared
poor Reynolds half to death."

"I honestly thought he could have done it."

"Don't be silly."

The woman was his own age, and yet he felt the way
he always had when he'd been chastised by his nanny as a
child.

"Beg pardon, sir!"

A white-haired man, an old salt judging by his well-
worn clothing and his rolling gate, had broken in on Hale's
thoughts with a mumbled apology as he jostled him on the
sidewalk.

What the— Hale was almost sure he'd felt the man's hand in his pocket. Frantic, he checked to see if anything was missing. On the contrary, he found a piece of paper with a written message in firm copperplate writing:

Madame Tussaud's, Jack the Ripper exhibit, 10 A.M.

Hale looked up to call after the man, but he was nowhere to be seen. *Well*, thought Hale, *I evidently have an appointment tomorrow morning with a person or persons unknown.* Normally only a fool would respond to such a summons, but Hale could think of few safer places than Madame Tussaud's to meet the mysterious individual who chose this peculiar way to demand an audience. The place would be crowded with tourists, and especially the area around the Ripper exhibit. What could go wrong in the Chamber of Horrors?

Monday morning did not start well for Hale. On his typewriter he found a note from Rathbone summoning him to the managing director's office. The tone of the missive was not warm: *See me. Rathbone.*

"Yes, sir?"

Rathbone looked up from his desk. "Close the door and sit down."

So, it's going to be that kind of meeting. Just as Hale had suspected.

"I understand that you have been making inquiries into the deaths of Lord Sedgewood and his son-in-law."

It could have been worse. Hale had been afraid that his boss had found out about Willie Gordon's contributions to his British Open stories. He could have gotten the sack for that.

"How did you know, sir?"

"Never mind how I know. Let's just say that certain people told certain people who told me. Did I or did I not tell you to stay out of that case?"

"You did not."

"Eh? Don't be insolent. Of course I did."

"With respect, sir, no you didn't. What you said was, 'You can't be reporting on a murder in which you're Scotland Yard's chief suspect, can you?' I acknowledged that I could not. But I haven't been reporting. I have merely been asking questions. I did, however, pass on some answers thus obtained to Ned Malone, who did report it."

Rathbone looked down, the trace of a smile at the corner of his lips, and fiddled with his curved pipe. "You know who you remind me of, Hale?"

"Someone good, I hope, sir."

"You remind me of me, damn it to hell." He paused. "Let me make this clear: I do not want to hear any more about you taking an interest in this case. Do you understand what I'm saying?"

"Perfectly, sir." Rathbone had said he didn't want to hear about it. He hadn't said "don't do it."

"Good." Rathbone lit the pipe, signifying that the stern-parent talk was over. "What do you have planned for today?"

"I was thinking about a visit to Madame Tussaud's."

"Tussaud's? The place has been around forever. Everybody's been there at least once. Where's the story in Tussaud's?"

"That's what I'm hoping to find out."

Madame Tussaud's wax museum had been founded on Baker Street by Marie Tussaud in 1835. Almost half a century later her grandson had moved it to its current location on Marylebone Road. Hale had visited the museum with Sarah once, viewing with special interest the wax figures Madame herself had created of Sir Walter Scott, Admiral Nelson, and victims of the French Revolution.

The museum was much more than that, of course, and not just wax. One of the current highlights was a collection of authentic relics of the Emperor Napoleon: three carriages, including the one he used at Waterloo and in the Russian campaign; his coronation robes; his toilet case and telescope; and the bed he died in on the island of St. Helena. The whole collection was valued at £250,000.

For the more gruesome-minded, however, the biggest attraction at Madame Tussaud's was and always would be the Chamber of Horrors, featuring such notorious killers as Jack the Ripper, Charlie Peace, Dr. Crippen, and Burke and Hare.

It was to the Jack the Ripper exhibit that Hale presented himself at ten o'clock, following the instructions on the paper placed in his pocket the night before. No one knew what Jack the Ripper looked like, Hale thought, but the aftermath of his horrific crimes was well attested to. Hale stood looking at the grisly tableau when he felt a hand on his shoulder. Thinking about it later, Hale turned red at the memory of how he jumped.

"Penny for your thoughts?" said a rough voice behind him.

Hale turned around quickly. At first he saw only the old sailor who had bumped into him the night before. Then the sailor stood straighter and, by some magic of control, altered his face. It was still an old face, but one that Hale knew well.

"Holmes!"

"I knew the Ripper, and so did Scotland Yard," he said quietly in his natural voice, nodding at the waxworks. "That is really quite a good likeness. The nose is a little too wide, though. Lestrade helped them with that figure. It was his charming way of letting certain people know that he knew without risking his own life."

The waxwork image of the killer didn't ring any bells for Hale. Possessing more than his share of the curiosity natural to every journalist, he couldn't help asking, "So—who was he?"

"That, I am afraid, is a story for which the world is not yet prepared, even after all these years."

"What's this all about, asking me to meet you here? And why the disguise?"

"At the request of my old friend Wiggins, who has little regard for Inspector Rollins, I have been making inquiries into the Barrington-Sedgewood murders. It's time that you and I share information about the case. However, I thought it inadvisable for Rollins' man who is following you to know that we are meeting. Incidentally, I hope you enjoyed your golf game."

"How did you—?"

"I followed you, of course, which is how I know that a Scotland Yard officer was also following you, and doing a fair job of it."

Hale felt foolish, as he often did in the presence of Sherlock Holmes. "I wasn't just playing golf. I was interviewing Sedgewood's butler, Reynolds." He told Holmes the whole story of his day on the links, starting with an abbreviated account of his earlier meetings with Agatha Christie, as they strolled through the Chamber of Horrors.

"Mrs. Christie should do well in her chosen profession of mystery writer," Holmes said at the end. "Her insight about the servants was spot on. I myself have been talking to the cook at Carlton House Terrace, a woman of about my age named Agnes. She is a fair hand at cribbage." His tone turned wistful. "I once knew a maid named Agnes. She married a baker. For a number of years I visited her husband periodically to make sure that he treated her well. Oh, look, my old friend Charlie Peace!"

As they stood in front of the waxwork representing the famous burglar and murderer, Hale worried—not for the first time—whether the years had at last caught up to Sherlock Holmes. He was reassured when the old detective got back on point.

"At first I was reluctant to leave Sussex and look into this business. My bees are demanding taskmasters, you know. But that was a mistake. By the time I saw how badly Rollins was botching the matter, it was far too late for me to explore the physical scene. Scotland Yard is fairly good at that sort of thing these days, anyway. I would make bold to say that they took a lesson or two from me. However, I did learn a bit from Agnes in the course of losing multiple hands of cribbage. Now, tell me what you found out, word for word if you can."

"I can." Hale pulled out a notebook that he had reserved for his jottings on the case. "I've been writing everything down after every interview, as much as I remember—and I have a trained memory. My involvement began with a phone call in the night from Ned Malone."

Hale left out nothing. When he'd finished quoting Harley Reynolds and closed the notebook, Holmes nodded thoughtfully. "You really have done quite well, Hale. You lack only the ability to draw conclusions from the facts you have marshalled."

"And I suppose you've solved the case already?" Hale didn't even try to keep the sarcasm out of his voice.

Holmes chuckled. "That would be saying too much, but I believe that I am making progress. In those detective stories that are so popular these days, the second killing is always The Man Who Knew Too Much. Sometimes in reality it does happen that a second murder is committed to cover up the first, but not so in this case. I am convinced that the killer framed Lord Sedgewood in the hopes of disposing of two people neatly—Alfie Barrington by knife and Lord Sedgewood by the hangman's rope.

"Think about it, Hale. Who informed the Yard about the murder weapon being the dagger if not the killer? And why do so if not to point to Lord Sedgewood, the owner of the dagger? It was a clever bit of misdirection, I must admit, except for the fact that it didn't work. When it became clear that Scotland Yard suspected the wrong person, the killer was forced to get rid of Sedgewood in a more direct way."

"Then you do know who the killer is?"

"I believe so, but because of your fine work I have a few more questions to ask before I can be certain."

TWENTY-ONE
The Baronet's Wife

"The worst of having a romance is that it leaves
one so unromantic."
> – Oscar Wilde, *The Picture of Dorian Gray*,
> 1891

Only with great effort was Sherlock Holmes able to
convince Hale that he, Holmes, alone should visit Lord
Sedgewood's friend Lady Lawrence and her husband, Sir
James Lawrence, Bart.

"I'm sorry, Hale," he had said, "but your connection
with the late Lord's daughter would make it impossible for
Lady Lawrence to speak honestly in front of you. Besides, I
believe you are under instructions from your managing
director to cease med— that is, to discontinue your
investigation."

"How the hell did you know that?"

Holmes merely smiled. He suspected that Hale
would have been upset to learn that he had been the one to
rattle Rathbone's chain—through Wiggins—about his star
reporter's unauthorized inquiries. Hale was a fine fellow,

both brave and intelligent, but Holmes was on the case now. And he knew more than he had let on to Hale.

He had written reports from his old friend about Carter ("apparently an honest mistake that His Lordship never forgave") and Baines ("a fraud, but everyone knows it"). He himself had learned much about Portia and Sidney Lyme, as well as all the members of the Sedgewood family, from the chatty Agnes. She had related with particular relish a rumor that Sidney Lyme, like Lord Sedgewood, had taken antiquities out of Egypt illegally. Since Agnes particularly specialized in low gossip, the name of Lady Lawrence was not unknown to Sherlock Holmes. All of the servants knew about her frequent visits and time alone with the master of the house.

She turned out to be a handsome brunette, taller than her husband. Although in her mid-fifties, she looked nowhere near her years. Holmes could see why Sedgewood would be taken with the woman. On this afternoon she wore a day blouse of a light blue silk Crepe de Chine decorated with a ruffle that ran in a rectangle down the front around a row of white buttons. Her mid-calf length skirt was a contrasting color of blue, and was embellished with a metal beading. These were not the clothes of a woman who skimped on fashion. Sir James appeared perhaps a decade older than Lady Lawrence, with a bald head and a distracted air. His attire reflected that of a man of a different age than his wife.

"Sherlock Holmes," he said, looking at the calling card bearing that name and nothing else. "Aren't you dead?"

"Not anymore," the beekeeper of Sussex said dryly.

"Oh, I see." But, clearly, he didn't.

"What's this about, Mr. Holmes?" Lady Lawrence spoke directly, but with no sign of irritation or concern. "You said on the phone that it had something to do with Lord Sedgewood."

"Yes." He hesitated. "I understand that you were quite good friends with His Lordship."

"Barely knew the fellow," Sir James said. "Seemed nice enough, though. Died the other day, didn't he?"

"I'm afraid so." Holmes looked at Lady Lawrence.

"I actually knew him better than Sir James did," she said. "We served together on a committee of the Arts Council."

"And your committee work required visits to his home?"

"On occasion." She turned to her husband. "I think this will be quite boring for you, my dear. Perhaps you would like to go back to playing with your trains."

"Wouldn't mind that at all. Pleasure meeting you, Mr. Holmes. Oh, wait just a moment, please." He dashed into another room.

As soon as he'd left, his wife turned to Holmes. "Is this some sort of attempt at blackmail? Because if it is—"

"Has my reputation sunk that low?" Holmes was more amused than offended. "No, Lady Lawrence, it is nothing of the sort."

"Here we are!" Sir James returned to the room with an autograph book in his hand. "Would you mind giving me your autograph? I collect them."

"It's one of his hobbies," Lady Lawrence said. "He has many hobbies."

"It would be an honor."

Holmes dashed off his signature and Sir Lawrence left the room.

His wife watched him leave. "I'm really very fond of him, Mr. Holmes. I wouldn't hurt him for the world."

"Nor have I any wish to do so."

She sighed. "I was an absolute fool to become involved with Edward—or any other man. James and I have been married for twenty-six years. It has been a very satisfactory arrangement. His hobbies keep him busy, and he has been very generous in supporting causes that are important to me."

"I perceive that you are an ardent supporter of Mr. MacDonald and his Labour party."

She appeared startled for a second, and then looked down at her blouse. Holmes gave her full marks for realizing that the small party pin had given her away. This woman may have been foolish, but she was no fool. Holmes had seldom regretted his long-ago decision to avoid affairs of the heart: They inevitably clouded one's judgment.

"You disapprove of women in politics, Mr. Holmes?"

"I disapprove of politics."

She arched an eyebrow. "But surely government is necessary or we shall have anarchy. And politics is necessary, or we shall have dictatorship."

Holmes could tell that Lady Lawrence enjoyed this verbal joust, and he was surprised to find that he did, too. Reluctantly, he judged the time right to bring up the subject that had brought him here. So instead of asking Lady Lawrence whether she thought that anarchy, dictatorship, and inescapably sordid politics were the only options, he said:

"Did you visit Lord Sedgewood on Friday?"

"You mean, did I kill him?" She put her hand on the top of a chair, as if to steady herself. "It didn't take a detective to realize that you must be investigating his murder. No, Mr. Holmes, I did not have that distinction. And I had not visited him since about two weeks before he was killed. Our last discussion was not a pleasant one."

"You had words?"

"It would be more correct to say that he had words. He summoned me to let me know that he loved another."

"No doubt you were upset." Holmes had learned from experience that others responded well to having their emotions acknowledged. The simple observation often caused them to talk more.

Lady Lawrence's free hand tightened. "Of course I was upset—for a good ten minutes. What woman wants to be told that a man is finished with her? I should have known that it was inevitable. I'd been told by one of his other women that he'd had many love affairs since the death of his wife, to whom he was apparently quite devoted. The worst part was that he offered me a financial settlement, for which I had no need or desire. That hurt."

"And after the ten minutes?"

"I realized that I was quite relieved that it was over."

"Because you didn't love Lord Sedgewood?"

"No, because I did. And he didn't deserve it. Nor did James deserve my infidelity." She sighed. "As I said, I played the fool—but not so big a fool as to kill Edward for leaving me."

Holmes couldn't claim to be a human lie detector, nor could any man. But he trusted his instinct that Lady Lawrence was telling the truth. He'd never seriously suspected her anyway. But he needed to be sure.

"Do you know the name of Sedgewood's new inamorata?"

Lady Lawrence gave a rueful laugh. "He didn't tell me that. Once, a month or so ago, I saw him dining in a discrete corner of Simpson's with a redhead, one of those wispy types. But it couldn't have been her—I later saw the woman with Edward and the rest of his family. He always kept his women separated from his family."

She folded her hands in front of her. "I'm afraid I haven't helped you very much, have I?"

"On the contrary, Lady Lawrence, you have been invaluable. I already knew with a fair degree of certainty who killed the Earl of Sedgewood. Now I know why."

TWENTY-TWO
Smuggling

Nemo sine crimine vivit (No one can live without crime).
– Latin Proverb

Portia Lyme!

Hale, dawdling over his feature story on Madame Tussaud's, suddenly sat up straight. It all seemed so clear to him now. Who would have a good reason to kill Lord Sedgewood? Portia Lyme! The woman who found the idea of a pharaoh's curse "just divine" might be impatient for her fiancé to inherit the earldom and the fortune that went with it.

And what about the murder of Alfie Barrington? Holmes undoubtedly was right that it was just the first step in a devious (or "just divine") plan to get rid of Lord Sedgewood. But was Portia Lyme really capable of such a round-about plan? *Never underestimate a woman.*

"Portia? Don't be silly."

Hale had hurried through writing the rest of his story ("Madame Tussaud's is an attraction that waxes but never wanes"), handed it in, and told a colleague that he was leaving for lunch.

He was delighted to find Sarah almost completely recovered back at her own home on Bedford Place.

"You assume Portia's not capable of murder?" he said.

"I suppose that I do assume that," Sarah said thoughtfully, "but that's not what I meant. Portia has no need of Daddy's money. Her family is richer than ours. And even if she did need money, and she was capable of murder, I can't see her killing Alfie and Daddy. Our families have been friends for years. Sidney and their late father, Sir Harry Lyme, used to knock about Egypt with Daddy."

Lord Carnarvon immediately came to Hale's mind. "You mean they were rivals at digging up the best mummies and that sort of thing?"

Sarah shook her head. "No, no, for some reason Sir Harry and Daddy were great mates. Maybe Daddy didn't feel threatened because Sir Harry was only a knight and not a peer. They helped each other out—and that's a good thing for Sidney. Daddy could have gotten him into a spot of trouble a while back if he'd chosen."

Hale felt the hairs on the back of his head rise.

"What do you mean?"

"Sidney tried to sell Daddy a marble *shabti* figure from the tomb of the High Priest Pinedjem I."

"What's a *shabti*?"

"It's a figurine of a servant, made out of clay or wood and buried with the body of an important person to assist him in the afterlife. This one should have been returned to the Egyptian government under the rules set up by the Department of Antiquities."

"You mean like that dagger your father shouldn't have had?"

Sarah frowned. "Not exactly. You see, unique items are supposed to go to the Egyptian Museum. The excavators are to divide the remainder, but only to go to public institutions and societies, like the British Museum or the Metropolitan Museum of Art in New York. But it's very common for excavators in Egypt to hold on to small items 'on account,' as they like to say. Rumor has it that Lord Carnarvon's widow had Howard Carter remove everything in her husband's collection taken 'on account' before she sold it to the Met so as to avoid embarrassment.

"Daddy's little dagger was easily taken out of the country and easily hidden away in his rather small collection in the townhouse. But the *shabti* figure that Sidney offered him was almost three feet tall, which put it into the Egyptian Museum category."

Hale rubbed his mustache thoughtfully. "Where is it now?"

Sarah shrugged. "I wouldn't know. I suppose Sidney still has it if he didn't find a willing buyer."

"And that could get him into trouble?"

"Only if—"

The doorbell rang. It was Inspector Rollins.

"Your timing is impeccable," Hale told the Scotland Yard official as they faced each other in the hallway. "I know who killed Barrington and Lord Sedgewood, and why."

Rollins smirked beneath his walrus mustache. "So do I." He held out his right hand. In it was a piece of old oilskin, which he unfolded. Beneath those folds was a golden-handled dagger. The hilt was an ornate gold palmetto design with what appeared to be semi-precious stones and on the copper blade was some floral device. (Hale had never been good at identifying flowers). "And this will prove it," continued Rollins. "Unless I miss my guess, tests will show that it was this wicked-looking instrument that ended Mr. Alfred Barrington's life."

Hale felt his chest tighten.

"Where did you find it?" Sarah asked in a wavering voice. Hale gave her credit for the bluff, even though it was a lost cause. Of course she knew where it came from, and Rollins knew that she knew.

"From your garden out back. We just dug it up. I knew there had to be some reason a stray dog's been sniffing around a patch of newly turned earth for several days now. My men have been watching. I'm hoping that we will find fingerprints on it." He refolded the oilskin. "Of course, the murderer may have wiped it clean, but you never know. We shall need to take the fingerprints of everyone in the household for comparison. I know you will have your servants cooperate. Oh, and I'll need yours and Mr. Hale's, of course, also. You understand that we must be thorough." The sneer in his voice was almost palpable.

With a sinking feeling, Hale knew that he was right about the fingerprints. Sarah wouldn't have bothered to clean her prints off of the dagger before burying it.

"Whose dagger is it, Rollins?" Hale asked.

"I believe it to be the rightful property of Queen Ahhotep, mostly recently to be found in the possession of the late Lord Sedgewood."

"Well, then, of course his fingerprints would be on it, and his daughter's as well," Hale said.

Rollins slowly nodded, apparently unmoved. "You may well make that argument at New Scotland Yard. But for the moment I'm taking you two into custody."

Lady Sarah made an inarticulate cry. Her hand went to her mouth and she collapsed against Hale.

"On what charge?" Hale demanded. The timing surprised him. He had thought Rollins would wait until after the formality of comparing the fingerprints to haul them in.

"You are both material witnesses in a homicide. That will do to hold you for the next seventy-two hours. Would you like to make this easier on all of us by just confessing now?"

TWENTY-THREE
New Scotland Yard

"Crime is common, logic is rare."
 – Sherlock Holmes, *The Adventure of the Copper Beeches*

New Scotland Yard sat at the end of Derby Street, on the east side of Parliament Street on the Victoria Embankment. The turreted building, in a Scottish design, was built on the foundation of what originally was going to be an opera house. Its granite façade was quarried, appropriately enough, by convicts at Dartmoor. Hale had been there dozens of times. Somehow, he reflected ruefully as he entered the building, it had looked different when he came there as a reporter rather than as a suspect in custody.

Of the 140 offices in the building, forty of them belonged to the Criminal Investigation Division. The Commissioner of the Metropolitan Police, Stanley Hopkins, had an office in one of the turrets overlooking the river. Senior officers, like Chief Inspector Henry Wiggins, had offices on the ground floor. The lower the rank of the inspector, the more flights of stairs he had to climb. Dennis Rollins's office, Hale knew from his most recent visit to the building, was on the third floor in an interior office that didn't even have a window onto the inside quadrangle. But Hale was quite certain that his ambitions fell nothing short of that turret office.

"You are each entitled to one telephone call," Rollins advised his charges unnecessarily.

Sarah wasted hers on telephoning Sir Edumund Featherstone, a stodgy old solicitor who undoubtedly excelled at wills and trusts but had never been involved in a criminal case. After giving the matter a good deal of thought, Hale decided to call no farther away than the ground floor of the building.

"Wiggins? This is Enoch Hale. Lady Sarah and I are enjoying the hospitality of Scotland Yard."

"I heard," the Chief Inspector said. "Rollins is quite proud of himself. But don't get too comfortable. You have friends in high places—or at least a friend of yours does."

"What do you mean?"

"I mean that you will be rescued within the hour. Just sit tight."

Never one to look a gift horse in the mouth, Hale gave up asking questions when it became clear that Wiggins preferred to keep him in suspense.

The same could not be said for Inspector Rollins. It seemed that he would never run out of questions as he sat across a table from Hale in a small, windowless room not far from his office on the third floor. Sarah sat on Hale's right. The initial interview would be together, and then Rollins planned to question them separately.

"When did you resume your relationship with Lady Sarah?" he asked Hale.

"I didn't. Not the kind of relationship you mean. We're friends, but until her husband died I hadn't spoken to her in any meaningful since her marriage."

"A witness says you were with her at an illegal after-hours club."

Hale shook his head. "I wasn't with her. We happened to be at the same place at the same time. It was a coincidence."

As soon as the word was out of his mouth, Hale knew that he shouldn't have used it. "Coincidence?" A malevolent smile appeared beneath Rollins's walrus moustache. "That's a good one. Is it a coincidence that with her husband and her father dead she's free to marry you?"

"Free to, is not the same as interested in."

"That's as may be, but what I really want to know is did she give you the knife or did you just take it?"

"She did nothing of the sort!" Hale had to hand it to Rollins; he had a way of getting under your skin.

"So you admit you took the knife without her knowing?"

Hale forced a contemptuous laugh. "I'd never even seen the thing before now. You won't find my prints on it. I didn't take it, she didn't give it to me, and for all I know you did it!"

Rollins half rose from his desk.

"Don't get cheeky with me, Hale. You're in this up to your neck." Sitting back down, he continued his interrogation. "All right, now, which one of you buried the knife?" Rollins surveyed the two potential murderers in front of him. Hale was trying to control his temper, but Lady Sarah sat with her shoulders humped and staring at her hands.

"One would understand, Lady Sarah, if someone like yourself should want to help an old flame. With your husband murdered and your old, *um*, friend in a desperate situation . . . well, it would be the most natural thing in the world to want to help out of fear of what the man might do next. A person might take the knife to hide it and hope she wouldn't be next. But now, with your father murdered too, well, you can see how it is. There is no safety from such a man. That's what happened isn't it? You hid the knife to help out Hale here because you were afraid for your own life."

Sarah didn't move. She just stared at the handkerchief she was twisting in her hands.

"I must give you points for originality on the story line, Rollins," said Hale. "But if I tried to turn that kind of no-fact drivel in to my editor I'd be working for the shilling shockers in two minutes. Look, somebody clearly has it in for the whole family. Sarah herself was poisoned. The doctor said she could have died."

Rollins grinned. "But she didn't, did she? The falsified attack is an old dodge."

Half an hour had passed and Hale was getting tired of this. He'd tried to tell Rollins that Sidney Lyme was the killer, but Rollins had ignored him.

"You don't really have anything, do you?" Hale said.

Ignoring that, Rollins pretended to study some papers in front of him. "Diligent investigation by the force has established that your friend Prudence Beresford doesn't exist."

"No, it just proves you can't find her," rebutted Hale. Rollins, not listening, pushed on.

"You have no alibi for the night Alfred Barrington was stabbed to death. Where were you when Lord Sedgewood, the man who rejected you as a son-in-law, had his head smashed in?"

"You don't even know when that was. All you know is when the maid found his body. I've given you a rundown of what I did that day four times—or maybe five. I may have lost count. But here it is again: I met the Woolfs at the 1917 Club, I interviewed Linwood Baines at his home, I went back to my office, I went out for dinner at Goldini's, I went home."

"Alone? Miss Beresford wasn't with you?" Rollins's voice dripped sarcasm.

"Yes, alone. Innocent people don't always have convenient alibis."

"Innocent people don't have murder weapons buried in their backyards." Rollins glared at Sarah, suddenly shifting the focus of his attack.

Hale was still thinking about how to answer that when the door opened. In his wildest flight of fancy, Hale would never have expected that the next person he saw would be Sherlock Holmes.

"Hello, Hale," the detective said briskly, as if he were the host of the party. "And you must be Inspector Dennis Rollins. My name is—"

"I know who you are," Rollins snapped. "I read about you when I was a nipper. That was a long time ago." *In other words*, Hale thought, *"you're long past it, old man." That's what Rollins means.* "What I don't know is by what authority you've come bursting into my interrogation of a suspect."

"That's interesting, because I was given to understand these people are being held as material witnesses, not suspects. In any case, your question is quickly answered." Holmes pulled an envelope out of his pocket and handed it to Rollins. "I am here by this authority—a letter to you from the Commissioner."

Oh, this is rich, Hale thought. He knew that Stanley Hopkins, Commissioner of the Metropolitan Police, and Holmes went way back together. Hopkins had worked with Holmes more than thirty years before, when the officer had still been wet behind the ears and Holmes was already the most famous sleuth in the world. Some of the Scotland Yard boys had been loath to admit how much they'd learned from the consulting detective, but not Hopkins.

Rollins opened the envelope, unfolded the single sheet of paper inside, and read it. Hale noted with satisfaction that he moved his lips when he read. After a couple of minutes, he lowered the letter and addressed Holmes.

"I suppose you've read the letter, so you know that Commissioner Hopkins wants me to extend you every courtesy and do whatever you ask within the bounds of the law." His moustache twitched as he spoke, as if in protest at what he was forced to say.

Holmes bowed his head in mock courtesy. "I believe that Commissioner Hopkins did tell me something of the sort."

Hale read the calculation in Rollins's eyes. Even though the young inspector had strong patrons, they weren't powerful enough that he could simply ignore a request from Stanley Hopkins himself—not if he planned to someday occupy that turret office.

"What can I do for you?" Rollins appeared to form the words with some difficulty.

"It's quite simple, really," Holmes assured him. "I should like you to bring together several individuals at the scene of Lord Sedgewood's murder. Rest assured, you need not leave Hale and Lady Sarah out of your sight during this charade. Their presence is quite crucial to exposing the real murderer."

TWENTY-FOUR
The Murder Room

They are greedy dogs which can never have enough.
– Isaiah LVI, 11, c. 700 B.C.

Lord Sedgewood's oak-paneled library felt different to Hale than it had when he was courting Sarah, even though everything looked just the same, save perhaps the addition of one or two minor items in the Egyptian collection. It wasn't just that the Earl was dead, never again to gaze upon his precious Egyptian artifacts, that had Hale disoriented. Rather, it was the inescapable realization that Hale had never really known the man who spent so much of his time here, even though Hale had thought he had.

"What are you shaking your head about?" Sarah asked. They stood together at the wall farthest from the fireplace, under the watchful eye of Inspector Rollins.

Your father was a womanizing scoundrel, Hale thought, *even worse a man than I imagined. And he thought I wasn't good enough for you!* "Nothing important," he said. "It just feels strange to be back here."

"Yes, it does. But this is the beginning of the end, isn't it? Holmes is going to end this nightmare, right?"

Sarah now looked none the worse for her time at New Scotland Yard. In fact, Hale found the glow of excitement that filled her wide green eyes quite fetching.

He squeezed her hand. "That's the agenda."

"Why doesn't he just tell us the name of the killer and be done with it?"

Hale smiled. "Because he's Sherlock Holmes, that's why. The man has an irrepressible flare for the dramatic. Remember the time he had his landlady serve up a missing naval treaty on a plate?"

"As a matter of fact, no, I don't remember that. I presume it was before my time. And I do hope he knows what he's doing."

"He's never yet been wrong in the end, when it really counted." *But what about those unsolved cases that Dr. Watson mentioned? Even Holmes failed there.*

Hale kept it to himself, but he worried that without knowing what he'd found out about Sidney Lyme's ill-gotten *shabti* figure, Holmes could be on the wrong scent. It was hard to tell, based on the *dramatis personae* Holmes had assembled in the library. Portia Lyme and her fiancé, the new Lord Sedgewood, stood at the unlit fireplace, deep in conversation with a man Hale took to be Sidney Lyme. Linwood Baines and Howard Carter stood on opposite sides of the room, studiously avoiding each other.

"Well, then," Rollins said, "everyone is here, so—"

"Actually, not everyone," Holmes corrected. He still cut a commanding figure as he stood in the center of the room, only a little stooped by age. "There's one more guest to come."

In a few minutes the doorbell rang and they were soon joined, to Hale's intense surprise, by a stout, elderly man he had seen briefly once before.

Holmes smiled broadly. "Ah, welcome, Watson." Hale gaped at the name.

"He called himself Burton Hill," Baines blurted out, obviously no less astonished.

"No hard feelings, I hope," Dr. Watson said, shaking his hand. "I apologize for the deception."

"It was quite necessary, I'm afraid," Holmes said briskly. "While I was stuck in Sussex, I needed an ally to begin the investigation for me. Not that I didn't trust Hale, but I strongly suspected that his emotions would bias his judgment in this case. My associate Mercer was unavailable, but my old partner Watson jumped at the chance to get back into harness. I could hardly allow him to use his own name without tipping my hand, could I? I'm afraid his rather sensationalized accounts of our adventures have been all too successful at spreading both of our names and linking them together forever."

"Right," said Rollins with ill-concealed impatience. "Now what?"

Holmes looked around the room. "Ladies and gentlemen, as you all know, Edward Bridgewater, the fifth Earl of Sedgewood, was murdered in this very room. His death was a particularly violent one, as he was crushed beneath a statute of the cat-headed deity Bastet." He pointed to a spot in the floor. "His body lay there, bleeding profusely from the head."

Sarah gasped and put her hands to her mouth. Hale put an arm around her waist, a natural gesture of comfort, without thinking about it. "Holmes! Please!"

"Surely," Holmes went on, "in such a circumstance the poor man's spirit cannot easily have moved on to a place of peace. It must linger here still, troubled and unhappy that his murder remains unsolved and the murderer unpunished. I suggest we attempt to communicate with this spirit."

"You mean a séance?" Howard Carter sputtered. "You can't be serious."

"Delicious!" Portia Lyme declared.

"Idiotic," her fiancé countered. Rollins somehow managed to agree with the new peer just by the look on his face, without saying a word.

Holmes turned to Sara's brother. Hale still had a hard time thinking of Charles as Lord Sedgewood. Holmes seemed to have no such problem. "You are skeptical, Your Lordship?"

"You're damned right I am. I don't believe in ghosties and ghoulies and things that go bump in the night."

"In short, you don't believe in the supernatural?"

Hale could have sworn that Charles's aristocratic nose turned up in the air. "No, of course not. That's just silly superstition. This is the twentieth century and I'm a rational man." In that moment Hale remembered Charles the day after Alfie's murder condemning *The Times* story with its "rubbish about Carnarvon and the supposed Tutankhamun curse." The family always read *The Times*.

"I wonder then," Holmes said quietly, "why you planted the idea of a curse in the mind of Mr. Artemis Howell of *The Times*."

Charles licked his lips nervously. "I did no such thing."

"I think you did. It has always been a habit of mine to closely read the Press accounts of cases in which I'm involved or interested. Although often inaccurate, I find such articles nonetheless instructive. Howell's story advancing the notion of a 'curse of Ahhotep' appeared the day after Reynolds overheard you expressing belief in such a curse to someone over the telephone. That someone was Howell. Most likely, you put the idea into his head to begin with. You were also his source 'close to the family' who told him about the acquisition of the Queen Ahhotep dagger."

"Nonsense." Charles managed to sound both contemptuous and superior in a single word.

"Why would he even do such a thing?" a bewildered Sarah asked.

"I can think of three reasons why a man might promote a theory he didn't believe in," Holmes said, "but the simplest—and therefore most likely—is to draw attention away from the real solution. Speculation about a curse, which even seemed to touch you in the form of a near-fatal illness, Lady Sarah, did more than evoke the supernatural. It also put a spotlight on the three victims' connections to Egypt. At least, that was the plan—although Inspector Rollins remained too focused on his own theory to see that. And why did the killer want to turn on that spotlight?"

"Because the killer had nothing to do with Egypt," Baines said with obvious satisfaction.

Holmes nodded. "Precisely. And who does that describe? Charles Bridgewater—he was the only member of the family who'd never been there or even taken an interest in Egyptology."

Sarah's body tensed, but she said not a word. Perhaps she couldn't.

Rollins and Charles both had their mouths open to speak, but Hale beat them to it. "That can't be right," he said. His own legs felt a little weak. "Sidney Lyme did it."

"Me?" Lyme looked bemused. He was much older than his sister, in his thirties, and portly in contrast to her slim figure. What remained of his hair was dark, whereas she was a redhead. Hale wanted to slap him and then shoot him. Instead, he shared what he had learned from Sarah:

"Lyme had an embarrassing secret to protect: Sedgewood knew that he had illegally smuggled a significant antiquity out of Egypt. I think he murdered to keep that secret."

"Come now, Hale," Holmes said. "You haven't thought that quite through. If Lyme wanted to kill Sedgewood to shut him up—and presumably Alfie

Barrington for the same reason—he hardly would have done so in a way that called attention to his Egyptian connections, the very source of his guilty secret! Besides, I learned about Lyme's smuggling from a certain female member of the household staff at Number 10 Carlton House Terrace, which means that it couldn't have been much of a secret."

Sarah pulled away from Hale, her arms out in appeal to Holmes. "But I already explained to Enoch that Charles didn't owe Alfie money. And he'd reconciled with Daddy. Why would he kill either of them?"

Holmes spoke with surprising tenderness to the woman who had lost her husband and her father in a matter of days, and whose brother now stood accused of the murders.

"As I explained earlier to Hale, your father was the real target all along. Partly it was about money, but nothing so trivial as a loan. Charles had an income from your father and was marrying a wealthy woman, but no man is satisfied with having money at the sufferance of others. He wants it for himself. As the only son, Charles would get that eventually—and a title besides—but that could be a long time coming. The Earl was in quite vigorous health—as he proved by making love to Charles's fiancée. That was the final straw, wasn't it, Charles—Lord Sedgewood?"

Portia Lyme seethed in the direction of her husband-to-be. "Are you just going to stand there and let him insult me like that?"

"As a matter of fact, I am, my dear. And thank you, Mr. Holmes, for providing all these witnesses for the lawsuit which I shall certainly file against you for slander."

Holmes appeared unmoved. "I regret the necessity to air these personal matters so publicly. It has been well attested by the household staff that the late Lord Sedgewood was romantically involved with a certain gracious lady who has learned her lesson and whose name need not be brought into this. She was succeeded in his affections by another whom she saw twice, once while the Earl was in the company of his family. Based on her description, the identity of this younger woman fairly leaped at me. How the current Lord Sedgewood knew about it, I have no idea."

"Oh." The word escaped Sidney Lyme as if he'd just realized he'd committed a minor social gaffe. "That might be down to my account. I was great pals with Alfie, you know, and I told him. It didn't seem cricket to me. Sorry, Portia. Alfie must have let it slip to Charles."

Lyme cowed before his sister, who regarded him murderously.

"So Charles had ample reasons to kill his father— too many, in fact," Holmes continued. "As the heir who had not so long ago been estranged from his father, he would have been the most obvious suspect, even to Scotland Yard."

Rollins glowered at Holmes.

"So, perhaps influenced by having once worked with the highly creative Dorothy Sayers, he conceived this rather convoluted plot of killing someone else, framing his father for the murder, and having the hangman clear his way to the title, the Sedgewood fortune, and Portia Lyme. That's been done at least twice before that I recall—in New York in 1895 and in Warsaw in 1913."

"But why kill Alfie, of all people?" Sarah cried. "Charles and Alfie were like brothers."

"So were Cain and Abel," Holmes said dryly. "I suspect that Charles loathed his brother-in-law for becoming your father's surrogate son during Charles's banishment from the family."

"No!" For the first time, the young peer showed emotion. "You think you're so damned clever, Holmes, but that wasn't it at all! I did it for Sarah. She deserved so much better than that buffoon Father talked her into marrying, someone who would appreciate her. Divorce was out of the question—she wouldn't hear of it. And even with Alfie dead, Father would have forced her to marry someone else just like him. So I killed Alfie with Father's precious dagger so that he would be blamed. You were right about that part, Holmes."

"And you put the dagger back in the library where you thought it would be easily found by the police," Hale said.

He nodded. "I did it when Sarah and I were at the townhouse the evening after I killed Alfie. But Sarah found it the next morning instead of Scotland Yard. She hid it to protect Father, and as a result the police suspected her. They just didn't understand what they were supposed to do." He glared at Rollins, who remained unmoved. "That's why I had to kill the old man. If they wouldn't hang him, there was no other way."

Sarah tore herself loose from Hale and started flailing at her brother. "You killed Alfie, you killed Daddy, and you tried to kill me."

Hale and Holmes pulled her off, while Rollins moved closer.

Charles dabbed a handkerchief at a bloody cheek. "I would never hurt you, Sarah. I pricked you with a small amount of nicotine to keep alive the curse idea and take suspicion off of you. No one would think you were the killer if you seemed in line to be the third victim. The nicotine turned out to be tricky stuff—just preparing it made me sick, and it made you sicker than I intended. But you weren't in any real danger. I insisted on calling the doctor when you didn't want me to."

Hale held Sarah as she cried into his shoulder. "How could he, how could he," she sobbed. Hale pulled her back from his chest and helped her to a chair by the open French windows.

"Mr. Bridgewater," said Rollins in his most officious voice, "I am placing you under arrest for the murders of your brother-in-law and your father."

Charles straighed up. "That's Lord Sedgewood, if you please."

"Not for long," Holmes said. "As a matter of fact—and law—I'm afraid you've no right to the title or the money that goes with it. One is legally prevented from gaining by a murder. Am I correct, Rollins?"

"Quite correct, Mr. Holmes." Rollins turned toward Charles. "Now, if you will come with me, sir."

Rollins placed his right hand on Charles's shoulder as he spoke. For an instant Hale saw the look he'd seen a thousand times in the eyes of men in the trenches during the Great War—that instant of panic and indecision when the officer's whistle blew and they knew they were to go over the top and face death. It was the animal instinct of fight or flight. Charles chose flight.

As Rollins touched him, Charles's right arm came up, clipping the Yard man under the chin. In the same instant, his leg swept from behind, catching the back of the man's knee and sending Rollins crashing to the floor. The inspector's head hit the hardwood with a resounding crack. The swiftness of the attack left the room stunned. Sarah and Portia were both screaming as Charles tossed a side table out of his way, rushing for the open French doors and freedom.

Hale didn't think; he reacted. As Charles passed Sarah's chair, Hale straight-armed the killer in the throat. Charles crumpled to the ground gasping for air, both hands clutching his neck.

My football coach at Yale wouldn't be very happy with that maneuver, Hale thought, *but it worked*. He smiled to himself.

Sarah jumped up from the chair and was in his arms once again, weeping as she buried her face in his chest. Hale looked over toward the fireplace where the Lyme siblings were trying to revive an unconscious Rollins. Holmes, he saw, was calmly charging his pipe. But then the detective's gray eyes widened.

"Behind you!, Hale!" he shouted.

Before Hale could turn around, he felt a hand grab his shoulder. As he spun to the right, a fist was laid on his chin, which sent him sprawling across the overstuffed chair and onto the floor.

Charles had recovered his feet while Hale had been taking his self-congratulatory bows. With fists still clenched, Charles turned again to the French doors and escape.

But there had been one more man in the room. Dr. John Watson now stood blocking the exit, service revolver in hand, the hammer cocked to the rear. Charles hesitated.

"I would suggest that you stop where you are." Watson's hand was steady. "I may be a little old, but I can still hit a target as large as you at eight paces. And if you are wondering, yes, it is loaded."

By now both Rollins and Hale had picked themselves up from the floor. Hale rubbed his chin and Rollins the back of his head. The unhappy inspector now scrambled to get his prisoner in handcuffs. There was no more of the burning energy in Charles's eyes now, thought Hale. No, now they were the sad, pitiful eyes of a captured animal.

TWENTY-FIVE
The Widow

"The course of true love never did run smooth."
  – William Shakespeare, *A Midsummer Night's Dream*, 1595

"I still can't believe that he did it for me," Sarah said a couple of weeks later. Hale thought she looked stunningly attractive in her black widow's weeds.

"Don't be so sure that he did. Holmes was probably right about the motives. He usually is. But let's face it"— Hale shrugged his shoulders—"who really knows? Maybe not even Charles. He may have talked himself into believing that his reason was a lot less selfish than it was. I guess it would take an alienist like, what's his name, Sigmund Freud to sort all that out."

Sarah wore an odd smile as Hale talked.

"Yes, Charles was a bit weak-minded at times," she mused.

They sat over cups of coffee at Simpson's in the Strand, their beef and pudding cleared away. It was the first time Hale had talked with Sarah since the day Rollins had dragged her brother out of Carlton House Terrace. She'd told him earlier that she had decided to sell the townhouse to the Union Club and live at Bedford Place for the time being. "The memories are better there," she'd said. "Not good, but better."

They had avoided talking directly about the murders over dinner, but the subject had lurked in the background until Sarah brought it out into the open as they drank coffee.

"Even if Charles did act out of some misplaced care for you, that's not your fault," Hale assured her. "No one is responsible for Charles except Charles. You might as well blame Dorothy Sayers on the grounds that he might never have conceived such a convoluted murder plot if he hadn't come in contact with her devious mind while working with her at Benson's."

Sarah smiled oddly again. "Well, I wouldn't want to do that. I quite liked Miss Sayers's book."

Hale shook his head in wonderment. "I never even suspected Charles, and I should have. Right after Alfie's murder, he said that your father was upset about Alfie hanging around with that decadent Bloomsbury Group, but that 'even the governor wouldn't kill a man for the company he keeps.' It's clear now that he was planting the seed for the idea that Lord Sedgewood did just that. And who would have wanted His Lordship to take the fall for Alfie's murder? The killer!

"Leonard Woolf gave me another clue when he said that Charles lived a fast life. I thought he was talking about ancient history, but Dr. Watson found out otherwise when he visited the Tankerville and Constitutional Clubs under the name of Burton Hill."

The Dr. Watson of Hale's imagination bore little resemblance to the gray-haired, thick-set gentleman who he had first met coming out of Linwood Baines's house. His image of the man, based on Frederic Door Steele illustrations of his writings in *Collier's Weekly*, was frozen in time.

"I think it will come out in the trial that Charles had a greater need of money than you knew about," Hale added. "I suppose that's another indication of his primary motive."

He decided that the subject needed changing. "What will you do now—return to the Alhambra as Sadie Briggs?"

"Not at the Alhambra, no." She looked at him and her eyes narrowed. "I'm going on a tour of the Continent, Australia, and the States. It's already booked. Has been for months. In fact, I leave tonight."

Hale was stunned. Even though Sarah had been somewhat reserved this evening, he had continued to hope that all they had been through together would lead her back into his arms. But that wasn't the only thing that jarred him.

"Wait a minute, Sarah. You've had a tour scheduled for months? Then you must have decided to leave Alfie before he died!" She had never hinted at such a thing in their previous conversations. "When? How?" His voice cracked with the confusion he was feeling.

As Sarah regarded him, her eyes had a coldness he had never seen before.

"You're getting your tie in the coffee, Enoch." Sarah sat back and took a sip of her own. "Really, is it all that hard to understand?" She put down the cup and waited for him to gather his thoughts.

"You really don't know what's happened, do you?" she said after a few moments. "I can understand that pompous Rollins not catching on, and Holmes is clearly past it, but I thought that you would have seen the whole picture by now. Well, you would have figured it out some day, I'm sure. It was just a matter of time."

"What on earth are you talking about?" Hale was starting to think that all the terror of the last few weeks had affected Sarah's mind.

Sarah leaned close to Hale across the table. Her eyes had become wild and her breathing quick. "Do you honestly think I could suffer to be married to that fool Alfie for any longer than necessary?" She looked around the restaurant to see that there were no other occupied tables near them and the waiters were at the service station before she continued. "And my licentious father—oh, sleeping around with any redheaded whore was fine for him, but I couldn't even sing on a stage, the family might be shamed!"

She leaned back a bit from Hale, an unsettling grin on her lips. "Don't look so stunned, Enoch. Do you think Charles was so hard to manipulate? He is now and always has been a loveable blockhead. He has no idea how the notion to kill Alfie and Daddy ever entered his head." She laughed. "It wasn't really hard, you know. Charles wanted to be rich and important. A suggestion here, a comment there, and he saw how to get there. With Daddy gone he would have money, he would have the title, and he would have Portia back. Simplicity itself. So he did just what I wanted and thought it was his own idea. I meant it when I said I still can't believe that Charles did it for me – but not in the sense that he thinks. How could I not adore him?"

"But he tried to kill you, too!"

"No, I'm sure he was telling the truth when he said he was just trying to make me ill to take suspicion off of me. Though, I must admit I didn't expect him, of all people, to have an original idea. But it didn't impress Rollins much, did it?" She finished her coffee.

His world turned upside down, Hale tried to make some sense out of what he was slowly accepting as a new reality. "Why did you bury the knife? You implicated yourself by doing so."

"Charles was entirely too subtle – the influence of that Sayers woman, I suppose. He wanted to merely frame Daddy and let the hangman take care of him permanently. That would never do; it was too uncertain. I knew that if I spoiled that plan, Charles would be forced to take a more direct approach. But I didn't expect the knife to be dug up from my garden." Sarah smiled. "I'm new at this, you know."

She stood up. "And now if you will excuse me."

Hale stood with her. Mad as it seemed, Sarah had just confessed to masterminding three murders—two by her brother and one by the Crown. He had to stop her.

"Oh, I know what you're thinking, Enoch. But it won't work, you know. There's no point in telling anyone else. I have done nothing against the king's law. It's not my fault that dear Charles got a crazy idea from a few casual comments of mine. But as I said, I must go. I'm catching the boat train at eleven tonight."

Hale watched as she picked up her wrap and purse. Opening the purse she removed a compact and lipstick. Using the mirror, she relined her lips and then slowly put the items back. Coming over to him she kissed him gently on the cheek.

"I couldn't have done it without your help, Enoch. Remember that before you get any ideas about going to the Yard. We would never hang, but bad publicity could be quite damaging to my career."

Turning, she started toward the door.

"Did you ever care for me at all?" Hale called after her.

She jerked around. "Of course I did, you ninny. I *wanted* you. You were part of my plan originally. But watching you play the sleuth, I saw that you're too good a reporter to be deceived permanently. And when you figured it out, you wouldn't have been happy with me, would you?"

"No." He could barely hear himself. His fists clenched without instruction from him.

"Do have a good life, Enoch," Sarah said as she threw her wrap over her shoulder. "I will."

As Hale watched the woman he had thought he had known disappear through the front door of the restaurant, two elderly gentlemen sat on the porch of a villa on the Sussex Downs looking out at the night sea. A three-quarter moon lit the cloudless sky. They watched the running lights of three or four steamers plying the white caps as they sipped sherry in the warm breeze. The decanter sat on the small table between them. Now and then each would add a bit to his glass. It had been an hour or more since either had spoken. Finally the shorter of the two men spoke as he charged his pipe.

"It doesn't seem right that she should get away with this, Holmes. Surely Rollins can charge her with something."

"With what—wishing someone dead? If that were a crime we should have all of England in prison." Holmes took another sip of the sherry before he continued. "No, wishing is not a crime."

"But she put the idea into her brother's head," responded Watson. "Or so you believe."

"She didn't do the deed, nor did she ask him to do it, nor did she conspire with him to do it. If she had, he would have turned against her at the end. And,"—he tapped the dottle from his pipe onto the porch flooring— "she was almost Charles's victim also. I do not believe that he meant to kill her, but it was a near thing. No, Rollins has no case against her that will play to a jury, even if he knows what she has done, and I doubt he does."

The two friends sat silent a while longer watching the running lights pass out of sight. Watson broke the silence again.

"And your friend Hale, do you think he knows?"

"Oh, no. He is a clever man, but love is indeed blind. I am quite sure he does not suspect at all. It will be interesting to find out what she tells him before she departs tonight on her world tour as Sadie the music hall singer. She isn't even waiting for her brother to hang."

"Sad, Holmes, very sad. I feel bad for the boy. If she doesn't tell him, should we?"

"The only way he would believe it is if it comes from her, Watson."

"Still, there must be something we can do."

"Oh, there is, old fellow, there is. We can catch her the next time around."

"The next time?"

"Oh, yes, Watson. We shall undoubtedly see her again."

The two friends returned to their silent thoughts and watched as the moon continued on its course across the darkened sky.

Notes for the Curious

This is an *historical* mystery novel, and as such blends facts and fancy, as in the two previous Enoch Hale novels. Once again, the locations are real and accurately described except for the Diogenes Club, the Drones Club, and the offices of the fictional Central Press Syndicate. The Drones Club was the creation of P.G. Wodehouse in his Jeeves stories. Some of the characters portrayed here have been historical, while the others existed only in the imaginations of the writers. For the curious, we present a few facts on the real life people who were involved.

Agatha Christie, DBE: Born Agatha Mary Clarissa Miller on 15 September 1890, Dame Agatha was an English crime novelist, short story writer, and playwright. She wrote sixty-six detective novels and fourteen short story collections, most of which revolve around the investigations of such characters as Hercule Poirot, Miss Jane Marple, and Tommy and Tuppence. Born in Torquay, Devon, she served in a hospital during the First World War, before marrying Archibald Christie, an RFC pilot, and starting a family in London. In 1920, The Bodley Head published her novel *The Mysterious Affair at Styles*, featuring Poirot. This launched her literary career. After her divorce from Christie, she later married Max Mallowan, an archeologist to whom she would remain married for the rest of her life. Christie's stage play *The Mousetrap* holds the record for the longest initial run: It opened in London on 25 November 1952 and is still running after more than 25,000 performances. In 1955, Christie was the first recipient of the Mystery Writers of America's highest honor, the Grand Master Award, and in the same year *Witness for the Prosecution* was given an Edgar Award by the MWA for Best Play. In 1971, she was made a Dame by Queen Elizabeth II. In 2013, *The Murder of Roger Ackroyd* was voted the best crime novel ever by 600 fellow writers of the Crime Writers' Association. Most of her books and short stories have been adapted for television, radio, video games, or comics, and more than thirty feature films have been made based on her work. She died 12 January 1976.

T.S. Eliot: Thomas Stearns Eliot was born in 1888 in St. Louis, Missouri. He would become a publisher, playwright, and social and literary critic. In 1914, he immigrated to England and in 1927 became a British subject. His friend Ezra Pound, another expatriate who appears in *The Amateur Executioner,* was instrumental in having Eliot's classic poem, "The Love Song of J. Alfred Prufrock," published in 1915. Eliot was one of the great poets of the twentieth century, and was awarded the Nobel Prize in Literature in 1948. Like most artists, his art did not make him wealthy, so he worked as a schoolteacher, a banker, and an editor. His first marriage was a famously troubled one. He died in London in 1965.

Howard Carter: Howard Carter was born on 9 May 1874, in Kensington, London. His father, Samuel Carter, was a successful artist. A sickly child, Howard was sent to live with his aunts in Norfolk. He was home-schooled, and was very artistic. When his father painted a portrait of a well-known Egyptologist, the young Howard's interest was sparked. He went to Egypt in 1891, at the age of 17, where he was to work on the Egypt Exploration Fund's excavation of the Middle Kingdom tombs at Beni Hassan. For several years, Carter worked under different archaeologists at sites including Amarna, Deir el-Bahari, Thebes, Edfu and Abu Simbel. He earned praise for using innovative and modern new methods to draw wall reliefs and other findings. Carter was hired by Lord Carnarvon in 1907. In 1914, Carnarvon received a license to dig at KV62, the site where it was believed the tomb of King Tutankhamen resided. He gave Carter the job of finding it. After years of digging, a boy who worked as a water fetcher on the excavation started to dig in the sand with a stick. He found a stone step, and called Carter over. Carter's crew found a flight of steps that led down to a sealed door and a secret chamber. On 6 November 1922, Carter and Lord Carnarvon entered the tomb, where they found an immense collection of gold and treasures. On 16 February 1923, Carter opened the innermost chamber and found the sarcophagus of Tutankhamen. The immense wealth of artifacts and treasures found in Tut's tomb took a decade to excavate. Howard Carter remained in Egypt, working on the site, until the excavation was completed in 1932. He then returned to London and spent his later years working as a collector for various museums.

Leonard Woolf: Leonard Woolf was born in London, the third of ten children of Solomon Rees Sydney, a Jewish barrister and Queen's Counsel, and Marie (née de Jongh) Woolf. After his father died in 1892, Woolf was sent to board at Arlington House School near Brighton, Sussex. From 1894 to 1899 he attended St. Paul's School (London), and in 1899 won a classical scholarship to Trinity College, Cambridge. In October 1904 Woolf moved to Ceylon as a government official. He returned to England in May 1911 for a year's leave. Instead, he resigned in early 1912 and that same year married Adeline Virginia Stephen. As a couple, Leonard and Virginia Woolf became influential in the Bloomsbury Group. Leonard's first novel, *The Village in the Jungle* in 1913, was based on his years in Ceylon. A series of books was to follow. As his wife began to suffer greatly from mental illness, Woolf devoted much of his time to caring for her—although he also suffered with depression/mental illnesses. In 1917, the Woolfs bought a small, hand-operated printing press with which they founded the famous Hogarth Press. Their first project was a pamphlet, hand-printed and bound by themselves. Within ten years, the Press had become a full-scale publishing house with a highly distinguished authors list. Woolf continued as its director until his death on 14 August 1969 from a stroke.

Virginia Woolf: Adeline Virginia Stephen, born 25 January 1882, was an English writer and one of the foremost modernists of the twentieth century. Between the great wars, she was a significant figure in London literary society and a central member of the influential Bloomsbury Group of intellectuals. Her most famous works include the novels *Mrs. Dalloway* (1925), *To the Lighthouse* (1927) and *Orlando* (1928), and the book-length essay *A Room of One's Own* (1929), with its famous dictum, "A woman must have money and a room of her own if she is to write fiction." She suffered from severe bouts of mental illness throughout her life, thought to have been the result of what is now termed bipolar disorder. She committed suicide by drowning on 28 March 1941 at the age of 59.

Ronald A. Knox: Born on 17 February 1888, Monsignor Knox was an English priest and theologian. He was also a writer and a regular broadcaster for BBC Radio. Knox, who attended Eton College, was ordained an Anglican priest in 1912 and appointed chaplain of Trinity College, Oxford. He left Trinity in 1917 upon his conversion to Catholicism. In 1918, he was ordained a Catholic priest. In 1919, he joined the staff of St Edmund's College, Ware, Hertfordshire, remaining there until 1926. Knox wrote many books of essays and novels. He explained his spiritual journey in two privately printed books, *Apologia* (1917) and *A Spiritual Aeneid* (1918). Directed by his religious superiors, he re-translated the Latin Vulgate Bible into English, using Hebrew and Greek sources, beginning in 1936. Knox wrote and broadcast on Christianity and other subjects. While Catholic chaplain at the University of Oxford (1926–1939), during which he was elevated to monsignor in 1936, he wrote classic detective stories. In 1929 he codified the rules for detective stories into a tongue-in-cheek "Decalogue," which is reprinted in this volume. He was one of the founding members of the Detection Club of London. His works of detective fiction include five novels and a short story featuring Miles Bredon, who is employed as a private investigator by the Indescribable Insurance Company. An essay in Knox's *Essays in Satire* (1928), "Studies in the Literature of Sherlock Holmes," was the first of the genre of mock-serious critical writings on Sherlock Holmes in which the existence of Holmes, Watson, et al., is assumed. Knox was led to the Catholic Church by the English writer G.K. Chesterton before Chesterton himself became Catholic. When Chesterton was received into the Catholic Church, he in turn was influenced by Knox, who delivered the homily for Chesterton's requiem Mass in Westminster Cathedral. He died 24 August 1957.

Sherlock Holmes: It is generally agreed that Sherlock Holmes was born 6 January 1854. William S. Baring-Gould speculated that his education was rather broad in that his family frequently traveled the Continent and he was exposed to many customs and languages. Early in his formal education he found that he had an uncanny ability to use inductive and deductive reasoning to solve problems. He decided on a career as the world's first consulting detective. In January of 1881, Holmes was just beginning to make a name for himself. But it was his meeting with Dr. John H. Watson that month that would propel his career into the stuff of legends. In more than twenty years of active practice the team of Holmes and Watson changed the face of crime fighting. Holmes retired from the field at a still-young age and devoted himself to the keeping of bees and the occasional mystery that he could not resist. His obituary has never appeared in *The Times* of London.

Ronald A. Knox's Decalogue of Detective Fiction (1929)

1. The criminal must be someone mentioned in the early part of the story, but must not be anyone whose thoughts the reader has been allowed to follow.
2. All supernatural or preternatural agencies are ruled out as a matter of course.
3. Not more than one secret room or passage is allowable.
4. No hitherto undiscovered poisons may be used, nor any appliance which will need a long scientific explanation at the end.
5. No Chinaman must figure in the story.
6. No accident must ever help the detective, nor must he ever have an unaccountable intuition which proves to be right.
7. The detective must not himself commit the crime.
8. The detective must not light on any clues which are not instantly produced for the inspection of the reader.
9. The stupid friend of the detective, the Watson, must not conceal any thoughts which pass through his mind; his intelligence must be slightly, but very slightly, below that of the average reader.
10. Twin brothers, and doubles generally, must not appear unless we have been duly prepared for them.

A Word of Thanks

The authors would like to offer their special thanks for the support of the following people:

Ann Andriacco

Steve Emecz

Bob Gibson

Jeff Suess

Steve Winter

They also thank Arthur Conan Doyle for creating Sherlock Holmes and Dr. John H. Watson.

About the Authors

Dan Andriacco has been reading mysteries since he discovered Sherlock Holmes at the age of nine, and writing them almost as long. His popular Sebastian McCabe—Jeff Cody series so far includes the books *No Police Like Holmes, Holmes Sweet Holmes, The 1895 Murder, The Disappearance of Mr. James Phillimore*, and *Rogues Gallery*.

A member of several scion societies of the Baker Street Irregulars since 1981, he is also the author of *Baker Street Beat: An Eclectic Collection of Sherlockian Scribblings*. Follow his blog at www.danandriacco.com, his tweets at @*DanAndriacco*, and his Facebook Fan Page at www.facebook.com/DanAndriaccoMysteries.

Dr. Dan and his wife, Ann, have three grown children and five grandchildren. They live in Cincinnati, Ohio.

Kieran McMullen discovered Holmes and Watson at an early age. His father, a university English professor, found his reading skills lacking and so, the summer of his eighth year, assigned him the task of reading the complete Doyle stories before school started again in September.

After a twenty-two-year career in the U.S. Army, twelve years in law enforcement, and twenty years as a volunteer fireman, Kieran turned to writing about his favorite literary characters, Holmes and Watson. His first book, *Watson's Afghan Adventure*, centers on Watson's war experience before he met Holmes. His subsequent novels, *Sherlock Holmes and the Mystery of the Boer Wagon* and *Sherlock Holmes and the Irish Rebels*, concentrate on the duo's wartime experiences. *Sherlock Holmes and the Black Widower* goes in a different and surprising direction.

Kieran lives north of Darien, Georgia, on a few acres with his Irish Wolfhounds and Percheron draft horses. He has three children and six grandchildren.

Also from Dan Andriacco and Kieran McMullen

 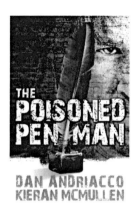

The Amateur Executioner

The Poisoned Penman

In contrast to most tales involving Holmes, The Amateur Executioner takes us into an ambiguous and murky world where right and wrong aren't always distinguishable. I look forward to reading more about Enoch Hale.

The Sherlock Holmes Society of London

www.mxpublishing.com

Also from Kieran McMullen

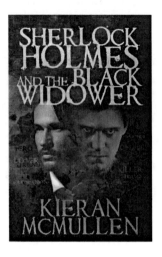

In the year 1908 Holmes believed himself to be in retirement. Watson was once again in private practice and unwed. Mrs. Hudson had gone to Sussex to act as Holmes's housekeeper. But the fates had agreed that Martha Hudson and John Watson should be together. Or had they? When Dr. Watson proposes to Martha Hudson it sets off a series of events that only Sherlock Holmes can deal with. Watson has already had three wives, all have died under unfortunate circumstances. Colm Campbell, Martha Hudson's nephew, thinks there is more here than meets the eye. Is Watson just unlucky or are the deaths suspicious? Holmes must come to his best friends defence.

www.mxpublishing.com

Also from Kieran McMullen

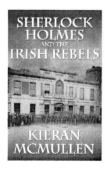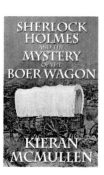

Watson's Afghan Adventure

Sherlock Holmes and The Irish Rebels

Sherlock Holmes and The Mystery of The Boer Wagon

Fewer people have considered the early life of John H Watson in any depth. Kieran McMullen, author of Watson s Afghan Adventure is a former professional soldier and a specialist in American military history an appropriate person to tell of Watson's experiences as an army surgeon. Exciting, and full of authentic military detail.
Sherlock Holmes Society of London

www.mxpublishing.com

Also from Dan Andriacco a modern mystery series;

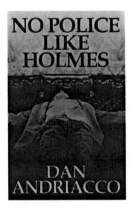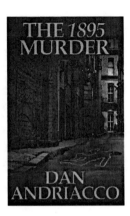

No Police Like Holmes, The 1895 Murder, Holmes Sweet Holmes, The Disappearance of Mr James Phillimore, Rogues Gallery.

"No Police Like Holmes" is an exciting and witty romp - not about Holmes but about his fans. The world's third-largest private collection of Sherlockiana has been donated to St Benignus, a small college in a small town in Ohio, and to celebrate, the college is hosting the Investigating Arthur Conan Doyle and Sherlock Holmes Colloquium. Jeff Cody, the college's PR director (and part-time crime writer), is an amused observer until the event is blighted by a real theft and a real murder, and he realises that there's rather a lot of suspects in deerstalkers. As if things weren't bad enough, Cody and his ex-girlfriend also become suspects... I like it!
Sherlock Holmes Society of London

Links

MX Publishing are proud to support the Save Undershaw campaign – the campaign to save and restore Sir Arthur Conan Doyle's former home. Undershaw is where he brought Sherlock Holmes back to life, and should be preserved for future generations of Holmes fans.

SaveUndershaw
www.saveundershaw.com

Sherlockology
www.sherlockology.com

MX Publishing
www.mxpublishing.com

You can read more about Sir Arthur Conan Doyle and Undershaw in Alistair Duncan's book (share of royalties to the Undershaw Preservation Trust) – *An Entirely New Country* and in the amazing compilations *Sherlock's Home – The Empty House* and the new book *Two, To One, Be* (all royalties to the Trust).

CPSIA information can be obtained
at www.ICGtesting.com
Printed in the USA
LVOW10s2343210318

570756LV00007B/102/P

9 781780 927763